RESCUE IN THE WILDERNESS

FRONTIER HEARTS
BOOK ONE

ANDREA BYRD

WILD HEART
BOOKS

ISBN-13: 978-1-942265-70-2

CHAPTER 1

NOVEMBER 11, 1779—ABINGDON, VA

Every fiber of William's being fought his presence in the room. His wandering feet itched to feel the soft, uneven terrain of a narrow game trail. His body craved fresh, untainted air and endless expanses of land, free of the confines of human society. Instead, his moccasin-covered foot bounced nervously on a hard wooden floor as he willed himself to remain seated among the sweaty, unwashed men as they imbibed spirits.

From his place in the corner of the tavern, he watched the room from under the brim of the leather hat that never left his head. Just as on the trail, his hazel eyes were ever scanning for danger. The crowd was unusually raucous—undoubtedly due to the sudden arrival of crisp fall air. The muscle across the top of William's shoulders rippled, and the hair on the back of his neck stood up, as if his body sensed something was amiss. An instinct he had learned to listen to.

He dropped a few coins on the table to cover his meal. But when he moved to stand, it was as if an invisible hand stayed him and kept him where he was. William's attention slid to the burly, red-headed Scot two tables away, who grew louder with every drop that passed his lips.

"Lucinda's birthday is of a morrow," he lamented miserably. "The lil' lass twill be a woman." The stranger banged a fist on the table then, and stood, his countenance suddenly resolute. "An' I need one o' ye men to take her off me hands!"

William's gaze cut to the man's red face, then to the crowd of unscrupulous men that cheered in response to the declaration. Their eyes gleamed hungrily as they hung on the Scot's every word. "A thorn in me side she has been. But I will play a table of ye men for her hand. An' ye can take her home tonight handfasted!" He thrust his pewter mug in the air, and though the amber liquid sloshed over the rim and doused his hand, he did not seem to take notice.

Hidden in the shadows, William's eyes widened a fraction as he considered the implications of the man's words. If the girl's father had his way, one of the drunk, belligerent men before him would take the poor girl home to do with as he pleased. And William's stomach roiled to consider what that might entail. Even now, the brutes acted as dogs, clamoring past one another for a position at the round wooden table where the burly man had produced a deck of cards. Two tall, slender brothers with matching sandy-brown beards scuffled over one of the wooden chairs and lost it to a short, stocky man with raven-black hair and beady eyes.

William warred with himself as the card game began. For the past four years, he had avoided human contact. He had fled south from Boston to a small colony in Virginia situated right outside the Appalachian Mountains and become a long hunter. Each year, he spent months at a time tracking game across the vast wilderness in and beyond the mountains. Alone. His only associations were ones made of necessity—those at the forts along what had become known as the Wilderness Road. Trips into town for the delectable fare at the tavern were a rare, special treat. Tonight, he had simply planned to fill his belly with warm, satisfying food before he headed out into the wilderness once more.

But instead, he found himself fighting the urge to flee straight to this woman and save her from the ill fate awaiting her. *Save her like I could not save Cora.* Pain shot through William's chest at the thought. His teeth ground together as the image of an empty bed, covered only in a new white sheet, flooded his brain. Then he forced his attention to return to two tables down. The red-headed ring leader was taunting the men with tidbits about his daughter. "Fair as the day is long. Just a wee wisp of a thing. Meek as a field mouse." William's brow knit together as an image of a young woman began to form in his mind.

Down the hill from the main village, near a tall stand of oak trees, there was a small, roughly hewn cabin. William passed it as he came and went from Abingdon. And sometimes, his gaze fell upon a pale, freckled face staring out the window. Her gray-blue eyes always held a longing that could be felt in the very depths of one's soul.

One memory pulled forward past the others. A mere year ago, he had happened upon the woman outside the cabin. The strangest scene had played before him as she had lowered the cup in her hand to the ground and allowed a small, grey field mouse to dash into the tall grass beside the cabin. William had stopped in his tracks as he watched the thin woman with his brow pulled together. In his experience, women normally screamed at the sight of mice and wished them dead. But here this ethereal young woman was, releasing one into the wild. Then, as soon as her gaze had locked onto his, fear had cloaked her entire being. Two halting strides had taken her to the door where she slipped inside.

William's heart constricted as he considered that face. Then his attention floated up to the middle-aged wife of the tavern owner as she brought another round of spirits for the eager men playing cards for the woman's hand. Or, at least, her virtue. Suddenly, William knew he could not stand by and let this happen. Whoever this Lucinda was, she did not deserve such a cruel fate. And William had enough on his conscience as it was. Maybe this would finally be a chance to redeem himself.

~

Lucinda sighed as the gathering dusk encroached on her view of the brilliantly hued oak and maples across the way. The beautiful palettes of gold, russet, and crimson held more fire and energy than the flames she had stoked in the rock fireplace that morning. Even through the pane of glass, it was as if she could feel the life that pumped through their broad leaves. Or, more aptly, the life that was slowly seeping out of them as the trees guarded themselves against the coming winter.

Her joints bore their own reminder of the cold snap everyone in Abingdon had awakened to that morning. Lucinda groaned as she flexed aching fingers to draw her worn wool shawl closer around her. Stretching her stiff back and wincing as tiny daggers of pain drove into her knees and ankles, she forced herself to shuffle over and stoke the fire once more. *Ne'er stop movin', my wee one.* Her mother's voice whispered in her mind and brought a small smile to her face. The vision of an angelic, blue-eyed face, framed by golden-blond hair, danced in the back of Lucinda's memory.

But her joy quickly crumbled as she gave the pot of stew another stir. Lit only by a handful of candles, the cabin had darkened along with the sky outside. The pitch black of night would be her only companion as she passed the endless hours awaiting her father's return. And while he had been furious when he left, he would likely return in a drunken rage. Since her mother's death ten years prior, it was his nature to be vile and violent.

Though, he had never been tender and loving like her mother. She touched a hand to her cheek where he had backhanded her the week prior. Waiting for his late return, she had accidentally fallen asleep and allowed his supper to cool. Lucinda had resolved to never make that mistake again.

So she took to the only task she knew could keep her

awake in the dim lighting—singing. Heeding her mother's advice, she marched painstaking circles around the kitchen table as she sang. If Lucinda could keep moving, she could stay awake. And though she was no singer, her voice as broken as her body, she conjured every word she could recollect from the memories of her mother's soft, lilting voice.

Lucinda entered an almost trance-like state as she focused her entire energy on the task. That was, until a banging on the door startled her from her song. Heart racing in her chest and a furrow in her brow, she whipped toward the sound. Never in her life had her father knocked on his own door. But she could not remember a time *anyone* had knocked on the door. Lucinda hesitated. Then, fearful her father was so drunk and belligerent he had forgotten all his senses, she rushed forward.

She had no more pulled the heavy wood ajar when it flew open and knocked her over. Her fingernails bit into the kitchen table as she caught herself and spun around, ready for another blow. But her gaze did not land on her father. Instead, a stranger stood in their home, his face carefully obscured under his wide-brimmed leather hat. "Who are ye," Lucinda asked, suddenly filled with dread.

"That does not matter right now. Are you Lucinda?" The voice that came to her from the shadows was a deep, husky one with a slight British accent.

Her eyes narrowed as she tried to glimpse some facial feature that might tell her if the man was trustworthy. But he kept his head carefully tilted even as he awaited her answer.

"Aye," Lucinda replied cautiously. Finally, the tall man

standing in the corner of the room lifted his head enough to chance a quick glance her way, and she caught a glimpse of his strong jawline above the black fabric wrapped about his neck.

"We need to leave. Now. Your father's at the tavern gambling your hand away in a game of cards."

Taking a step backward, Lucinda gripped the edge of the table behind her. *It cannae be.* She shook her head emphatically as tears formed in her eyes.

The stranger took a step closer. "I have no reason to lie to you. How else do you reckon I knew your name?"

Lucinda turned away and squeezed her eyes shut. The man's argument held validity. Her father never spoke of her to anyone. She was an embarrassment he kept carefully hidden within the four walls of their cabin. "What else did he say?"

The stranger took an audible breath. "That you will be a woman tomorrow, on your birthday. He plans to handfast you to whoever wins and send you home with them. Tonight. He described you as fair and slight in frame."

Lucinda ventured another glance at the man standing before her. She sensed he was not telling her everything, that her father had said more. But for some reason, this broad man, clothed in a wool shirt and fringed deerskin coat and breeches, seemed to want to protect her. *Why?*

"An' what will ye do with me? Will ye have me for yerself?" Lucinda raised her chin and crossed her arms.

"No." The stranger's response was immediate. "But I will help you escape. We will hide at Black's Fort tonight, then I will take you on to Anderson's blockhouse. You can decide how far you want to go from there. I am going through the Gap into Kentucky to hunt."

The breath left Lucinda's body, and her lips parted at the possibility. Never before had she envisioned any kind of future for herself. She had resigned herself to the prison her father had created for her. In some ways, she had even believed the lies he fed her about no one wanting to see her hideous fingers, her uneven gait, or the multitude of freckles across her paper-white cheeks. He had told her that her gray-blue eyes were the work of the devil. But Lucinda knew better.

Her gaze went once more to the stranger before her, to his downcast face and the worn leather hat obstructing her view. Did he turn away because the view was so repellant? She sensed not, sensed that he had his own secrets. And something within her was beginning to trust this man whom she felt might be a kindred spirit. Had God brought him to her? Was God offering her a chance to be free of this place?

As soon as hope worked into her soul, it was bit back by fear. What would it mean to leave? Where would she go and what would she do? Sure, she could keep a house. But that was the extent of her abilities. Plus, any potential employer might balk at the sight of her.

Again, her mother's voice came to mind. *Follow where the Lord leads, my dear. He will always take care of you.* Lucinda's breath hitched and excitement rippled through her.

She started to step toward the stranger but stopped when he spoke. "We need to hurry if we are going."

Lucinda stepped back. "Oh. Right." Had she just made a decision?

If what this man said was true, her father would return any minute with the intention of handfasting her to whichever drunk man happened to win her hand. And to make their getaway, they would have to escape unseen.

Lucinda moved to the trunk at the end of her bed and dug out an old bag. Inside it, she shoved a single change of wardrobe, her mother's Bible, and her shawl. Then, biting her lip, she added a handful of other items that might be of necessity. Last, she pulled her mother's old coat from the chest and held it up. With a knot in her throat, she slipped on the wool garment before she turned back toward the stranger.

"Is that all?" The question came from across the room.

Lucinda nodded. She owned little else. The stranger crossed the small cabin in a few easy strides, but she withheld her bag when he reached for it.

Instead, she looked squarely up into the shadowed face of her rescuer. He was easily a head taller than her and, from her position, she could see under his carefully placed shield to the whiskered edge of his profile. Her eyes trailed along the curve of his jawline to the corner of his mouth, then up and over his ear to the sandy-brown hair that appeared golden in the glow of the fire. An odd urge swept through her, to reach up and touch his face, to remove his hat and reveal all he kept hidden. But she resisted the urge and settled for one important piece of information. "If I am to travel with ye, I wish to know yer name."

"It is Cole. William Cole." As soon as the words left his

lips, he bent forward, retrieved her bag from her grip, and ushered her toward the door. Lucinda stumbled over her own feet as she was propelled forward. And then, without warning, she was outside. Frigid air slammed into her face and took her breath away. William glanced in either direction, then turned to her. "You all right?"

Lucinda nodded. "Aye," she breathed, and the action brought forth a small cloud in front of her face. She had never been so cold in her life. But for the moment, she was quite happy about that fact. "Let us go." She gave another little nod, a grin on her chilled face.

William turned and took the lead as they embarked on their short trek to Black's Fort, located just outside of town. Light from a full moon filtered through the trees and lit their way in silvery streams. Before she knew it, they had arrived at the shallow bank of the narrow Wolf Creek.

"Jump," William advised after he had tossed her bag safely across.

Lucinda hesitated. What might the icy water feel like should she come up short? But when she took the leap, William Cole's strong hands came up to grip her small waist and gently propel her forward. Though her joints protested her landing, she arrived on the other side no worse for wear. Then she turned and watched as William took the creek in a single leap. With one hand on his hat and a small grunt of effort, he was once again by her side.

Minutes later, they were standing in front of a strangely shaped building, its dark wood shrouded in the dark of night. Lucinda cocked her head to the side as she stared up at the front of the large fort house, whose second story was wider than the first. She stood, lost in the marvel of it, while William took one last look over his shoulder and knocked on the door.

Despite night being full upon them, an answer came immediately. A broad, dark-headed woman peeked around the door, gun in hand. Then, seeing William, she discarded her gun against the wall and ushered them in with a warm smile. "Come in. Come in."

"Lucinda needs a safe place to stay tonight. We will leave out before first light," William explained as soon as the door was closed behind them. How strange. The man before her was comfortable in his element. He did not hide his face from the dark-haired woman as he did with Lucinda.

"Of course. Come in, come in. Josiah is down with a cold or he would have met you. He still tried but I shooed him back to bed." She waved a hand as she moved to allow them into a room the full length of the building with a fireplace at the center. The robust, healthy-looking woman disappeared from the room and returned with a plate of bread and cheese and a cup of water for Lucinda. "Eat, my dear, while I fetch you some furs for your bedding." Then she was gone again, leaving Lucinda to settle at the small table next to the door. William hovered nearby, lingering in the shadows cast by the light of the oil lamp at the center of the table.

Lucinda had no more sated her grumbling stomach, than the dark-headed woman returned with an armload of furs. She stopped and nodded to William Cole, who dropped to one knee. Carefully, he lifted a section of floor that, only moments before, had appeared completely contiguous with the other boards. Lucinda's hand stopped on the way to her mouth. "Time to head below, my dear. It is a mite cold and dark, but you will be safe. Just knock if you need anything."

Lucinda moved over and peered down into the darkness. At her hesitation, William offered a hand. She slipped her fingers onto a large, strong palm covered in a leather glove. "It is only four feet down," his deep voice advised seconds before her feet touched earth.

Then, furs were being handed down and Lucinda took them graciously. "Thank ye." She smiled at the other woman before the section of floor was returned over her head. With a sigh of contentment, she settled herself into a cocoon of furs and whispered a heartfelt prayer of thanks for the change of circumstances. And for the first time she could remember, she fell asleep eager to see what the day ahead held.

CHAPTER 2

*L*ucinda awoke the next morning to the sound of scraping boards above her head. She peeked out from her nest of furs to find William Cole peering down at her. Lamplight silhouetted his frame as he extended an arm down to assist her up.

"Time to go." His voice carried the deep huskiness of early morning. The warm sound, combined with excitement for the day's journey, coursed through Lucinda. Without hesitation, she placed her hand in his and allowed him to haul her up. Her slight frame felt featherlight in his strong hands. "Mary has some things for you in the kitchen," William advised as soon as her feet touched the floor. His hat-covered head inclined toward the room into which the dark-headed woman had disappeared the night before to fetch bread and cheese.

Lucinda gave a nod and then stiffly limped toward the door. With her joints still waking, she was glad to hear the scuffling sound of William replacing the section of board behind her. At least he was not staring at the pitiful sight of her rigid, broken gait.

In the other room, she found the dark-haired woman, her smile as broad as the night before. "Come, have a seat, my dear. I made a warm breakfast for you." Mary slid a tin plate onto the table in front of a roughly constructed chair. Atop it was a scrambled egg and a couple precious slices of still-sizzling bacon. Lucinda's eyes widened at the sight.

"Thank ye." She settled at the little round table and shoveled a forkful of eggs into her mouth before she turned her attention to the older woman.

"I knew you would be needing some warmer clothing for your travels, so I went through my Elizabeth's things and found you some wool stockings and such." Mary patted one side of a leather saddlebag. "She was done a mite bigger than you when she married, so she left them behind when she moved north with her husband. But for now, Mr. Cole thinks it would be best for you to dress as a man. At least until you are away from here. So I took in some of my husband's things for you to wear." Now the woman's hand rested atop a folded stack of garments.

Lucinda blinked up at Mary. "You did all that last night...for me?"

"'Twas nothing." The other woman gave a wave of her hand, then gestured toward her plate where half a piece of bacon still lay untouched. "But we best be getting you on your way."

Lucinda nodded, reminded as to why they were leaving before sunup, and shoved the bacon in her mouth.

"I will let you change now. Will you be all right on

your own, or do you need help?" When Mary's dark eyes met her own, she was surprised to find no judgement, only concern.

"I can manage." Lucinda smiled and waited for her to exit before she approached the pile of clothes. She could not remember the last time she had changed in front of someone, and she certainly had no desire to do so now. Her body was an embarrassment. The fingers that rested atop the gray wool fabric were hideous. Her index finger and middle finger were exceptionally longer than the others, and they all bent at an awkward angle toward her thumb. And that was not even to mention the larger-than-normal joints.

Lucinda sighed as she reached for the button on her skirt. The rest of her figure was just as unsightly. Every rib was visible due to malnourishment, and her right leg was longer than her left, just enough to leave a hitch in her gait. But then there were the scars. The long lines that, though she could not see them, she knew were there. Should someone run their hand along the flesh of her back, they would feel what her father's utmost rage could do to her frail body.

Pushing back tears, Lucinda hastily changed. Then she sat at the table with her hands clasped and waited for the soft knock that belonged to Mary Black. "I am ready," she called, and stood for the other woman to enter.

Mary looked her over before she met her gaze with a warm, satisfied smile. "Such a shame to hide all that beauty. But I think it will do just the trick in case you encounter any trouble."

"Beauty?" Lucinda could not keep the shock from her voice. Her brows drew together.

"Of course, my dear. Why, such a fair little thing as yourself, I would not be surprised if you do not end up a married woman by the end of your journey." Mary winked at her, but Lucinda simply stared in bewilderment. *Married?*

"But, I am—"

A knock on the kitchen door interrupted them.

"We are decent," Mary called across the room.

Lucinda turned to see Mr. Cole step through the door. And though his face remained hidden under his hat, she could feel his gaze as he assessed her attire. She looked down at her feet and tugged at one sleeve on the men's jacket. Though Mary had done a wonderful job of making the clothing fit well enough to stay on, she was still so thin that the fabric hung on her like a burlap sack.

"That will work." William finally nodded. "Are we ready to go? I have the horses out front and dawn is already breaking."

At the urgency in his voice, Lucinda's heart began to beat double time. She faced Mary, who bustled forward with the saddlebags. The woman led the way out into the semi-dark, where she helped secure everything to the saddles. She patted the bay on the shoulder. "I told William to choose two of our best. He always borrows horses from us when he heads west." She met Lucinda's gaze, her face serious, then enveloped her in a tight hug. "Be careful, my dear. And I pray you find God's place for you in this world."

Tears stung Lucinda's eyes as she blinked them back.

"Thank ye for everything." It broke her heart to leave when she had found such a kind, accepting soul. But she knew it was not safe to stay within reach of her father.

"Have you ever ridden before?" William glanced her direction as Lucinda moved to mount her horse.

She paused, her left hand holding her reins and the pommel of the saddle. "A verra long time ago," she replied, her voice breathy as she was reminded of long-forgotten memories. Painful memories of life before her mother passed. Of being seated atop a big black horse in front of her father. That had been before he realized what a disappointment she was. Lucinda pushed the memories back where they belonged and raised her chin. "But I believe I remember how." As if to prove her words, she slipped her left foot in the stirrup and managed to vault herself up into the saddle.

William watched her for a second before he easily swung up into his own saddle. Meanwhile, Lucinda stared at the ground, which, in the early-morning shadows, seemed miles away. And much like herself, her horse was as thin as a rail. She felt as if she were precariously perched atop a skinny ledge and the slightest of breeze could send her toppling over the side. Still, when William's mare walked forward, Lucinda asked her own horse to follow. *I can do this.*

A line of light purple was visible on the horizon as they started out, and with each step their horses took, the sky became lighter. Trees started to take shape on either side of the trail ahead of them as they travelled through a short, open valley. Lucinda had begun to settle into the soothing rhythm of her mount when a shout made her eyes pop open wide.

"Hey!"

William reined his horse in and turn toward the sound. She followed his gaze to where several men on horses had picked up a lope at the sight of them. With each lingering second, they grew closer and her hope of freedom grew smaller. William moved up beside her, close enough that she could feel his strong calf against hers through the borrowed linsey-woolsey pants. A shiver ran up her spine. "Walk on as if everything is fine. As soon as you are over that ridge, ride as hard as you can, as long as you can. When your horse starts to tire, walk on a little farther, then hide in the trees and wait for me."

Lucinda swallowed before she gave a tentative nod and nudged her horse to walk on. Cold spread over her calf where William's leg had rested, and a chilly breeze swept against her face and neck, causing her to shiver as she moved on without him. But she did her best to focus ahead, on the approaching rise in the landscape, rather than the sound of hoofbeats behind her as William rode down to meet what was likely a search party. When her horse's shoulder rippled beneath her, Lucinda grabbed onto the saddle horn. Likely, her mount sensed her anxiety. She took a deep breath and leaned forward to run her hand over warm muscle covered in chocolate-brown hair.

After what seemed like several minutes, she and her mount crested the ridge. She turned to make sure they were out of sight, then lifted a prayer. *Lord, please protect William and bring him safely back to me.* Lucinda's breath hitched. The prayer seemed intimate for two people who barely knew one another. But she did not want the man to encounter any harm on her behalf, and she would be lost without his guidance.

Trusting in William's advice and God's protection, she urged her horse to run. Lucinda grabbed at the saddle as the thin bay lurched into a lope. Then, as she settled into the rocking gait, she kissed to the gelding and squeezed with both legs to urge him on. Her heart beat wildly as the ground flew by beneath them. The horse's hooves seemed to thunder on the hard earth, and she prayed it was a sensation only she could hear. For she did not dare look back to see if anyone followed. Instead, she focused only on staying in the saddle.

At the bottom of the hillside, Lucinda's eyes widened when a creek seemed to spring up out of nowhere a couple paces in front of them. But in a single bound, her agile gelding gathered his haunches under himself and launched for the far bank. Not ready for the jump, Lucinda was whipped backward, then forward. When they landed with a creaking of leather, her left foot came free of the stirrup, and she slid sideways. Her horse threw his head and let out a snort as she grabbed a handful of black mane to right herself. Then, in another flash, they were through the small grove of trees and in a broad meadow.

The sun was fully over the horizon, and a warm, early-morning glow lit the dew-dampened grass on either side of the path and made the leaves all around the valley sparkle in bright, fiery colors. Cool air brushed against her face as they sailed over the ground. It pulled her hat from her head to flop against her back and loosed her hair from its pins. Lucinda reveled in the sensation. A joyous laugh left her body as her blood coursed through her veins. For the first time in what seemed forever, she felt alive.

~

A jittery impatience grew within Lucinda as she waited for William to emerge on the other side of the meadow. With what seemed all her willpower, she kept her body rooted to the ground where she knelt next to her horse. The tall, skinny bay foraged lazily along the forest floor, searching out bits of grass in the growing carpet of dead leaves, as she held the end of one rein. But she could not seem to tear her gaze away from the opening at the far side of the meadow. It seemed as if hours had passed since she and her horse had ridden through that very place.

Endless thoughts raced through her mind as her stomach swirled with anxiety. Had William been hurt by those men? Was he hanging from a tree or lying dead in a ditch somewhere because of her? The images that surfaced in her mind made her grab for the nearest tree as she forced the contents of her stomach back down. How would she ever live with herself if William died trying to set her free? Tears welled in her eyes as she started to regret her own selfishness.

But then, something above the far tree line caught her attention. She squinted past her tears at the thin wisps of black smoke that swirled up into the air. As she watched, the plume transformed into a rolling cloud of obsidian and slate. Lucinda's heart squeezed. Something was desperately wrong. She bit her lip as she glanced at her horse and back again.

Should she go back? Was there anything she could do to help? Lucinda's shoulders sagged. She was a frail, useless nobody. She would likely be a hindrance rather than a help. But still...how could she sit by and do nothing?

Just as she was about to turn and mount her horse, a flash of color at the edge of the meadow caught her attention. Relief flooded over Lucinda as her heart lifted. *William.* She would recognize that light-golden mare anywhere. All the air exited her body as she gathered up her reins and stepped out from the tree line, into view. She watched William's strong form as he confidently loped his horse across the meadow. The man coming her way did not hide his face. He sat tall in the saddle, his attention affixed to where he wanted his horse to go. Lucinda tried to scan for a reason he might have hidden his face from her before but, from a distance, she could only see a handsome man that took her breath away as he rode.

Lucinda swallowed and averted her gaze. Even if she could marry and have a family, she could never garner the attention of a man. Her eyes were dull, her skin as pale as the clouds above, and her cheeks covered in a spattering of unsightly freckles. Not to mention her physical abnormalities.

"Are you all right?" William's voice jerked her from her thoughts as he reined his horse in.

Lucinda nodded. "An' ye?" She scanned over his body for injury but did not attempt to meet his eyes.

"No worse for wear. But they burned Black's Fort."

Lucinda's hand flew to her mouth as she gasped. Her eyes snapped up to William's face, and under the shadow of his hat, his mouth set in a grim line.

"Mary and Josiah made it out and disappeared into the woods unseen. They will be all right," he assured her. Even so, her heart squeezed in her chest. Had they lost their home because of her? "The search party believed my story but thought you might be hiding there and tried to smoke you out." He shook his head. "They are not the brightest group. Looking to make mischief more than anything. I do not think we have to worry about being followed."

Lucinda nodded. At least they had that to be thankful for. But as she remounted, her thoughts were still with Mary and Josiah Black. If the cost was already this high, would their journey truly be worth it?

CHAPTER 3

William's jaw worked as he watched Lucinda sleep within her fur pallet, still curled in the fetal position she had taken up the night before. Her thin face was pale, but the furs rose and fell with her soft breaths. Still, concern knit his brows together. Daybreak was long since passed and yet, the woman had not stirred. Not even the smell of biscuits and salt-cured ham warming over the fire had enticed her from her slumber.

But her fatigue was not nearly as worrisome as the pain he had seen etched on her face the night before. While a day spent in the saddle could make any inexperienced rider sore, the lines on Lucinda's beautiful face had run deeper than that. As she handled what needed tending to, she had moved with the grace of an eighty-year-old woman after a life of hard living. Then, forgoing supper, she had sank into the position she lay in now.

Finally, William cleared his throat. No movement. He frowned and tried again, louder. When she still did not stir, he let out a growl of frustration. A man should not have to work this hard to wake his woman. William let out another growl—this time at himself. The beauty lying beside him was not his any more than the reddish-brown oak leaves that skittered across the ground each time the wind blew. And she never would be. No woman would want to be with a beast such as him, plagued by scars inside and out. The same familiar guilt rose up to gnaw at his conscience.

William shook his head and refocused on the task at hand. Though he could not save his sister, he now had the opportunity to save Lucinda. And he would do everything in his power to see that she made it to safety and freedom. Clearing his throat yet again, he all but bellowed her name.

With a start, she stared up at him, eyes round and wide. His chest squeezed at the sight. Her beautiful blue-gray eyes held all the fear of a field mouse cornered by a tomcat. When Lucinda blinked at him and cocked her head to the side, he realized he was staring into her freckled face straight on. William tipped his head down and indicated the plates of food he still held in his hands. "Time to eat and be on our way."

"Aye. Of course." She shook her head at herself and bolted upright. A tiny whimper of pain left her when her left wrist bore her weight momentarily. But she cleared her throat, presumably to hide the sound.

"Thank ye," she whispered, her own head ducked as she accepted her plate.

~

*T*hough her knees, ankles, and lower back all felt as if someone had lit flaming torches of pain within them, Lucinda did her best to enjoy their surroundings as the sun began to lower in the sky. A pleasant breeze cooled her cheeks and tugged at the loose strands of hair around her face and neck. William had agreed it was safe for her to don her own clothing now that they were over a day's ride away, but she had elected to keep the wide-brimmed hat that protected her face from the sun. She smiled as she recalled their encounter that morning when she walked back into camp and asked if he thought it was acceptable attire for a woman to wear.

William had let out a deep chuckle that warmed her insides and lifted the corners of her mouth. "Plenty of women don wide-brimmed hats on the trail," he had conceded. "But you might want to turn yours around." His tall, sturdy frame had stalked right up to her and plucked the hat from her head, spun it around, and settled it back. "Perfect," he had whispered huskily before he went back to packing up camp.

It seemed such a silly little gesture for him to fix her hat, but Lucinda's mouth had quirked up at the corner for the rest of the morning. And somehow, her energy to start the day had been restored. Though her body ached, the Lord had blessed them with another beautiful day on the trail. *And another adventure with this valiant man.* She could not help the grin that spread across her face as she watched the back of the strong long hunter who rode in front of her.

Without warning, William stopped his horse on top of

a hill and allowed her to ride up next to him. Lucinda obliged and urged her horse to halt alongside the palomino mare. When William raised his arm and pointed to a small meadow to their right, she followed his gaze. Along the tree line, seven deer stood grazing amid the tall grass in the fading afternoon sunlight, completely oblivious to their presence. "Not something you see every day in town, is it?"

Lucinda smiled at the reverence in William's voice. "Nay," she agreed. Though she did not admit that it was something she had never seen. Her eyes misted as she took in the beautiful sight of the graceful animals living freely in the world God had created for them. Lucinda's heart ached to feel that same freedom. To find the place that He had created for her.

"Not much farther to Anderson's blockhouse." William took in the lay of the land, then asked his horse to walk on.

Lucinda nodded even though he could not see. She frowned as they settled back into their rhythm and the deer bounded into the safety of the trees.

Though she had travelled with William for two days, she was not sure any of their interactions could be considered an actual conversation. Not since they left her father's cabin. And though it was as much her fault as his, he piqued Lucinda's curiosity more than ever. That morning, she had captured a glimpse of the face he kept so carefully hidden. His eyes were a warm hazel that complemented the sandy brown of his hair and beard. They had been friendly and focused on her with concern and compassion. They had roped her in so much that she had almost forgotten to search out the rest of his face. But before he tipped his head down, Lucinda had caught sight of some sort of marring across his skin. That was what caused him to hide his face? It had not seemed so bad.

Just who was this man, William Cole? Her brow knit and her mouth twisted as she peered now at the back of his tan leather coat. His squared shoulders exuded confidence and capability. The fringe hanging from his coat seams swung gently with the rhythm of his palomino mare. And his chin was lifted under his worn, ever-present hat as his eyes scanned the horizon for trouble.

Lucinda knew two things to be true. She may not know William well, but she trusted him with her life. And with both their lives, she trusted God. She had to. She could not bear one more person suffering on her behalf.

❧

"There it is." William nodded, his hat indicating a structure at the edge of the river valley they were about to enter.

Lucinda's eyes widened and her heart kicked into a higher speed as she took in the large blockhouse and the dozen tiny encampments surrounding it.

When she had envisioned Anderson's blockhouse, it had been similar to that of Mary and Josiah Black. Safe, secure, and inhabited by a single, kind couple whose child had already grown and started a life of her own. She certainly had not imagined the thirty or so people that loitered outside—an audience waiting to ridicule her and her lopsided gait. *You are a pathetic insult of a human being.*

Her father's words returned to her and suddenly, she could not breathe.

Seemingly sensing her hesitation, the bay beneath her halted. William rode a stride or two farther before he turned in the saddle, as if he, too, could sense her insecurity. He came back and stopped next to her, but she could not tear her eyes away from the crowd below. Her heart might beat right out of her chest, or else fail from overexertion. The tips of her fingers and toes began to tingle.

"Lucinda?" William's voice was gentle yet belied his concern. The sound snapped her attention to him, to the comfort she found in his presence and the strength of his wide shoulders.

"I...I cannae..." Lucinda's round eyes darted to the blockhouse and back. Desperately, she sought the face behind the hat. Her heart longed for the reassurance that would certainly be in those hazel eyes.

Instead, William's shoulders sagged. With realization? "How long were you hidden away in that cabin?"

Tears sprang into her eyes, both at the tenderness in his voice and the memories that surfaced as a result of his question. "Nearly eleven years," she whispered, barely able to hold herself together. "Since my ma died." Lucinda squeezed her eyes tight, but it did not stop the flood of pain.

The day they buried her mother was bleak and cold. A sudden wintry snap had left a heavy frost on the ground and a deep ache within her joints.

"Pa, I hurt," she had whined with tears in her eyes. Her mother had always been the one to comfort her, and her hopeful heart had wanted him to do the same. But instead, he had lashed out. A giant hand had swung around to back-hand the side of her face.

"Cause yer a child of the devil," he had raged, his eyes full of hatred and contempt. "Ye took yer mither from me, an' ye will rot in hell for it."

Lucinda's body shook as she recalled the heartbreak that had torn through her little, seven-year-old frame. In that moment, she had become painfully aware of the fact that she was utterly and completely alone in the world. Her one friend and confidant in life was gone, to be placed in a grave that very day. And since that day, she had never complained to another person about her pain.

Not that Lucinda had much chance. Within a matter of days, they had left home and headed south, settling on the outskirts of the Virginia colonies. Someplace where her father could hide her away from the public eye.

For over ten years, she had been a prisoner and slave to her father, with her weak faith as her only solace. Until William Cole had burst through her door.

She looked up at him, tears still rimming the edges of her eyes. And when he took a deep breath, for one split second, she thought she would face his betrayal as well. That he, too, would decide she was unworthy.

Instead, he swept the hat off his head. Lucinda's mouth opened. Underneath his shield, William's face was covered in pockmarks. Her heart went out to him and bound with his as she realized that she had been traveling with a soul who knew her woes. Suddenly, she understood why he hid his face. People could be cruel and unkind. Her father was the perfect example.

But as her eyes skimmed over the lines of his face,

Lucinda felt only warmth for the man in front of her. While some might not consider him handsome, she did. To her, the small marks scattered across his face were nothing. She saw past the imperfection to the strong jawline, set and waiting for her disappointment. And to the tortured hazel eyes that shared some of the same pain and fear she felt within her own soul. The brownish-gold mixture of hues that showed compassion and understanding, and let her know that, for the first time in nearly eleven years, she was not alone.

"If they can accept me, they can accept you," William finally whispered. He fit his hat back to his head and raised his chin, determination filling his stance as he looked her in the eye. "And if they do not, they will have to deal with me."

True joy bubbled up inside Lucinda and spread across her face. She gave William a small nod to signify that she was ready to continue on. Alongside him.

CHAPTER 4

William was aware of Lucinda's deep, steadying breaths as the two rode into camp side by side. He shared the same trepidation within his own being but kept it under check. Lucinda needed him, and now he understood, at least partially, why. So he faced forward with his chin high as they rode through the ocean of curious eyes to the hitching post near the door of Anderson's blockhouse. Once he had the horses tied and their girths loosened, he moved over next to Lucinda, whose feet were still firmly planted where she had dismounted. Her eyes were downcast, and her arms wrapped around her body protectively, her petite hands carefully tucked under her elbows to hide their disfigurement.

William placed a reassuring hand on her elbow, his fingers brushing with hers as he did so. The act sent a pleasant shiver through his body. Instinctively, he stepped closer, until there were mere inches separating their bodies. Lucinda's face came up to meet his, her eyes round and nervous, her pale lips slightly parted. "The Andersons are good people," he reassured her.

Her head bobbed in a tentative nod before he wrapped an arm around her slender waist and guided her toward the door. William attempted to ignore how perfectly she fit against his side, her small frame melding perfectly with his. He cleared his throat and relinquished his grip as he ushered her inside the blockhouse.

"Cole! Aren't we glad to see ye?" John Anderson noticed his presence immediately and came over to grip his arm in a friendly greeting. The man's gaze swept over to Lucinda and back, his broad smile turning mischievous. "An' ye have a beautiful lass on ye arm this time!"

William chuckled at the other man's enthusiasm. "Lucinda. Um, Miss..." He motioned toward her as he fumbled through his brain for her surname. *Did you ever ask her?*

"Gillespie," she interjected.

"Yes. Miss Gillespie here needs protection." He faltered. "And possible passage west." Suddenly, his chest ached with the realization that the woman next to him might not be traveling on with him. He had offered to bring her this far and allow it to be her decision whether she continued on.

Lucinda nodded and gave him and John a small smile, but nothing in her blue-gray eyes gave away her intentions.

When Rebecca Anderson came scurrying up, William decided to take his leave. "I will tend to the horses while you get settled," he said, with only a glance in Lucinda's direction. Then he made his escape, filling his lungs with the crisp, fresh air. Outside, there was no beautiful damsel in distress that affected his better judgement and made him feel like more than he was.

~

*L*ucinda watched William's retreating back with the sinking feeling that she had been fed to the wolves. But a brunette woman with a kind face and a red-headed toddler on her heels had already taken her hands into hers. "I am Rebecca. An' we will be glad to have ye for as long as ye need to stay." She winked at Lucinda as she led her over to a bench situated in front of the large stone fireplace in the center of the room. "Have a seat, an' I will ladle ye up a bowl of stew."

When her stomach growled in response to the hearty smell that wafted to her from the pot hanging over the fire, Lucinda blushed. Rebecca did not seem to take notice of the sound as she hurried off to fetch a bowl, so Lucinda closed her eyes and relished the warmth of the fire against her weary body. She stretched her feet out in front of her, placing them as close as she dared to the flames. It was a heavenly feeling, and she prayed it would ease the ache within her joints.

"Here ye are," Rebecca offered moments later.

Lucinda peeled open her eyes and smiled as she accepted the bowl. "Thank ye. It smells delicious."

"Well, I pray it tastes as good." She shot Lucinda another wink. Her deep-brown eyes reflected the golden glint of the fire and made her appear all the more jovial.

"Just eat up, an' we will tend to what is ailing ye as soon as ye bones are thawed."

The limp. Lucinda's heart fell along with her face. "'Tis nothing that can be fixed, Mrs. Anderson," she replied quietly, the words difficult to force past the lump in her throat.

Their hostess was quiet for a moment before she came and settled on the bench next to her. Her knee brushed up against Lucinda's through their skirts, hers a vibrant mulberry and Lucinda's a dingy gray. Rebecca placed a comforting hand on her arm and waited until she lifted her gaze. Warm, sympathetic eyes met hers.

"Call me Rebecca. An' I am sorry. I did not mean a thing." She shook her head and squeezed Lucinda's arm. "We are used to tendin' a heap of injuries around here, an' I assumed ye limp meant ye had been injured on the trail."

Lucinda bit her lip and shook her head.

"Is there anything I can do for ye, though?" Her brows lowered, and her mouth thinned into a line. "Mr. Cole said ye need protection."

Lucinda's heart thudded in her chest. She had not shared her woes with another soul since the day her mother died. Even William only knew what he had learned from the pub, from her father himself. Could she risk sharing now? Rebecca Anderson seemed like a caring, accepting woman. And the familiar Scottish accent that lingered in a second-generation immigrant such as herself created a certain kinship. She warred with herself as the conflicting emotions rose up inside. Then, when she opened her mouth to speak, the opening of the block-house door caught their attention.

"I found a couple of familiar faces," William announced as he threw the door open wide.

Lucinda gasped at the sight of a bedraggled Mary Black leaning against a tall, dark-headed man she could only presume was her husband, Josiah.. The sound was quickly followed by the cry of a babe in the background. Rebecca jumped up to comfort the infant but stopped to lay a hand on Lucinda's shoulder.

"We will talk later," she advised quietly.

Lucinda nodded before she sat her own bowl of stew aside and rushed to Mary's side. Tears blurred her vision as she embraced the woman she barely knew but who hugged her back with the strength of a relation. Actually, Lucinda did not remember ever being squeezed so tightly. *Maybe when Mither was alive.*

"I am so sorry about yer home," she cried into the other woman's shoulder.

Mary pulled back and held her at arm's length. Her eyes belied her weariness, but the smile on her face was genuine. "Do not fret over a thing, my dear. I am only glad to see you made it here safe and sound."

Rebecca returned a moment later with her infant cuddled into her shoulder. She bounced, shushed, and soothed all while she welcomed the newcomers into her home.

Moments later, a stocky red-headed man with a fur cap entered the cabin. "There you are, my dear." Rebecca beamed up at him and planted a kiss on his lips before she turned and introduced him to Lucinda. She gave a nod before, with a quick gesture, Rebecca instructed John and William to move additional chairs next to the fire so everyone could properly warm themselves. Then she whisked the tiny toddler at her heels off to a place to the side where he could stack wooden blocks only to knock them down.

Lucinda smiled at the flurry of activity as she gathered up her unfinished stew and returned to her place at the end of the bench. Mary and Josiah settled into mismatched wooden chairs to her right, while Mr. Anderson took up the straight-backed chair at the opposite end. William glanced around, then selected the opposite end of the small bench.

Before she knew it, all newcomers held a bowl of warm stew and Rebecca was looking to sit down. "Mr. Cole, if ye would not mind to scoot down, I will have a seat here next to me husband." She squeezed her husband's hand and gave him a playful wink, to which he responded with a warm smile. Outwardly, it seemed the action of a loving couple. But as William obliged, Rebecca caught Lucinda's gaze with a mischievous gleam in her eye. Lucinda nearly missed the action as she attempted to keep her eyes down and focus on remaining out of everyone's way.

A blush crept up into her cheeks as William scooted close enough that his shoulder rubbed hers each time he took a bite of the hearty stew. And as Lucinda looked around at all the friendly faces, her heart was full. A genuine smile tugged at the corners of her mouth. For the first time in her life, she was in a room full of people who accepted her as she was and did not detest her presence.

Tears of joy stung her eyes, and she blinked them back before anyone could notice. *Thank ye, Lord.*

"We are expectin' Robertson to return any day now to lead this latest Kentucky-bound group gatherin' outside the fort. But they could use another gun along." Mr. Anderson broke the silence as he addressed William. His hair was a russet color, and he spoke with a confidence and familiarity that made difficult conversation easy. "Ye know it is always smart to have extra hands that know the way."

Lucinda glanced up at William to see his jaw set and his mouth form a thin line. But he nodded in understanding, the brim of his worn leather hat dipping minimally with the small gesture. He was the only one that kept his hat on inside, though no one seemed to notice or mind. "I will be ready when he is," William confirmed. "But Miss Gillespie has not yet decided how far west she will go."

He turned to her, his hat not even brushing the top of her head as he did so, for he was so much taller than she. Lucinda found it difficult to breathe with his full attention focused on her, the firelight flickering in his golden-brown gaze. His sandy brows arched in question, but she could not form an answer.

Rebecca saved her. "We were goin' to discuss that later."

Lucinda glanced down at her empty bowl as the heat of another blush rose up her neck. "Aye," she managed.

The answer seemed to settle the matter for the men because Mr. Anderson then turned a similar question to Mr. Black. "Have ye considered whether ye an' Mary be travelling west with the group?"

The man whose dark hair was peppered with white gave a sad smile. "I am afraid we have too many years behind us for such a journey. If it suits you and the wife, we will rest here until I can find a way to rebuild."

Mr. Anderson nodded his consent, then resumed the conversation as if nothing had occurred. There was discussion of how many guns were in the crew and when they would leave out. Thankfully, the arrival of Mr. Robertson still would not mean they would leave immediately. Apparently, there was much that went into mobilizing such a large group and guiding them into hostile territory. And that meant she would not have to make her decision directly. Lucinda glanced at William out of the corner of her eye, and her heart clenched.

If things were different, she would not hesitate to follow him into the wilderness of central Kentucky the two men spoke of. For some reason, her being longed to be near him. Maybe it was simply the comfort she had found in his presence over the past couple of days. Surely, she could develop that same comfort with any accepting soul? Rebecca and Mary were prime examples of that.

But the truth was, she would be a heavy burden to the travel party. An added risk with nothing to contribute. As the men conversed, she learned the journey could easily take a month or more depending on travel conditions, with few stops for supplies. They were truly heading into unsettled territory. Could there truly be a place for her there?

And more importantly she could not go forming attachments to men, even handsome long hunters who stirred something within her soul. For that could prove more dangerous than braving mountainous heights and the savage wildlands beyond.

~

"*F*inally asleep." Rebecca exhaled a deep breath later that night as she reached the bottom of the ladder that led to the second level. "If that 'un don't keep me on me toes, his brother does. But I could not imagine me life without 'em." She waggled a finger in their direction as she spoke, then settled into her seat and took her warm cup of tea into her hands.

Lucinda blushed as Rebecca looked between her and Mary. The world had long since gone to sleep, but the three women sat up at the little table near the door, an oil lamp in the center lighting their faces. Rebecca's hand left her cup and reached out to grip Lucinda's in a reassuring squeeze. She never seemed to notice Lucinda's deformed hands. "Dinna fash yeself. Everythin' will stay between us." She glanced at Mary, who nodded.

Resolve strengthened by the old Gaelic phrase her mother used to use, Lucinda swallowed and began. "William...Mr. Cole...rescued me from me own home. Me father was gamblin' my hand away at the tavern. An' he was goin' to send me home with the winner that verra night, handfasted."

A sound of disapproval came from Mary's direction, while Rebecca took a sharp breath.

Lucinda continued to stare down at the brown liquid in her cup. "Mr. Cole said he would bring me this far. Then, it is me choice if I go on, through the Gap." When no one spoke, Lucinda raised her eyes. But much to her surprise, she found no judgement in the faces that stared back at her, only shock and sympathy.

"Lucinda," Rebecca began after a moment. "Did ye father...abuse ye?"

Lucinda's heart beat faster, and her eyes darted downward. She gave a slight nod. Another sharp breath from Rebecca. She sighed and forced more words past her lips. "He...blamed me for me mither's death. An' he thought me an invalid, an embarrassment...a curse from the devil." A tear slipped down her cheek, and Rebecca's hand squeezed hers again.

"Ye know it is not true, right?" There was no hesitation in Rebecca's voice as she responded.

Lucinda gave a reluctant nod. It was not the truth of God, her God. But she still struggled not to believe the words she had heard day in and day out. Her father's degrading voice had become a part of her own subconscious, a constant companion that stayed put with or without her permission. Always there, always reminding her of her faults and shortcomings.

"Do you know what it is that ails you?" Mary's soft, tender voice pulled her from her inward spiral. Lucinda hadn't heard such empathy since her mother passed. She shook her head.

"Nay. It ailed me mither as well, though not so much. She looked normal an' walked without a limp. Best I can remember." Her eyebrows bunched together as she fought to locate memories that had been pushed to the back of her mind. "I think hers came with age, an' that is why he blamed me. But she caught the ague the winter I was seven an' dinnae make it through." She shook her head as tears tried to push past her lashes.

"Well, it does not matter." Rebecca's voice was strong, but there were tears in her eyes when Lucinda met her gaze. "Yer beautiful, just the way ye are. An' ye deserve to live a full life. If God blesses ye with breath in ye lungs an' life on this earth, ye should make the most of it. Live it." Her dark-brown gaze bore into Lucinda's, and the conviction with which her words were spoken made Lucinda's heart pound in anticipation. Suddenly, adventure and a life well lived danced before her. Possibilities she had never dared to dream of began to take shape within her mind.

Mary was the one to break the silence. "So that leaves one question. Are you staying behind or following Mr. Cole through the Gap?"

Lucinda looked between the expectant faces in front of her and took a deep breath. Before she even realized her answer, a smile tugged at her lips. And the other two women answered with grins of their own.

CHAPTER 5

$\mathcal{W}$illiam gritted his teeth as a makeshift choir lifted the chorus of a hymn heavenward from somewhere in front of Anderson's blockhouse. Hymns always seemed to work their way into his soul and convict him for the faith he had so recklessly thrown by the wayside when he learned of his sister's passing. He let out a groan and pushed his hat down on his head before he stood.

From the position where he had set up camp, behind the blacksmith forge and away from everyone, William could watch the service without notice. He scanned the faces of those in the congregation, as he had done several times that day. For one face. Lucinda's. But disappointment washed over him once more when her strawberry-blond hair and pale, freckled face were nowhere to be seen. With every passing moment that she remained holed up with the Andersons, his chances of accompanying her west grew slimmer and slimmer. Why would anyone choose to endure the hardships and dangers of the trail alongside the likes of him when they could stay within the safe, warm confines of the blockhouse with Rebecca's friendly smile?

Though, for the life of him, William could not understand why he cared what decision Lucinda made. She would be a liability at best. But as soon as the thought entered his mind, guilt washed over him. That was not true. He had ridden with Lucinda for two days. He had witnessed her strength and resolve. Sure, she had her pitfalls. What person among them did not? But despite the pain that had been evident on her features, she had not once complained or voiced her discomfort. And whatever limp she carried, it had not prevented her from keeping up with him, even that first night on foot. No, William felt deep within his heart that the woman was stronger than any of the women gathered in the meadow for church. For Lucinda had been forged in fire, heated and manipulated by circumstances no one, particularly the young and helpless, should ever have to face.

William's heart ached at the thought, and without realizing he had taken a step, he was headed for the blockhouse. Paying no mind to the preacher, who had started his sermon a mere twenty paces away, William walked with purpose. His gaze remained fixed on his destination —the front door. He stalked through small encampments and past hides stretched to form shelters and then marched right through the door without faltering. Immediately, he regretted his decision.

Rebecca's bright, friendly gaze met him from the corner of the room, where she had their littlest one nestled in a cradle, rocking it with her foot as she read her Bible. Though her eyes crinkled with a smile as William stepped inside, she held a finger in front of her mouth to remind him to remain quiet. He gave a nod and surveyed the open lower level. A fire crackled in the large stone fireplace in the center of the room, but no one else was in sight. After creeping quietly over to a chair, as if he were approaching wild game he planned to take down, he settled at the little table along the left front wall.

After what felt like an inordinate amount of time, the floorboards creaked overhead. He turned toward the ladder which led to the second floor. When no one made their way down, he craned his neck in an effort to see upstairs—nearly upsetting his chair in the process. William jerked and grabbed onto the table. As he settled the wooden legs back on the floor, a quick glance revealed Rebecca had not been disturbed by his silent shenanigans. A small wave of relief washed over him before his attention returned to the shuffling noise above his head. Someone was definitely stirring, someone whose footsteps carried the weight and sound of a petite woman.

At the sudden sight of a familiar gray skirt billowing over the top of the ladder as its owner started downward, William leapt to his feet and all the breath left his lungs. In seconds, he was at Lucinda's side. His large hand found a spot at her slender waist where he could support her in case she fell. When she reached the bottom and turned toward him, his hand remained in place. Suddenly, the woman he had been waiting all morning to see stood mere inches from him, surprise reflected in her blue-gray eyes as she stared up at him.

Without his permission, the left corner of his mouth tipped up in a grin. "Good morning," William whispered huskily. Then, he mimicked Rebecca's action by holding up a finger before she could respond. He tipped his head in the direction of the woman and child as an explanation. Lucinda's thin pink lips form an O, and she nodded in understanding before she allowed him to guide her outside. The preacher was still going, wagging a finger in the air as he delivered a spirited sermon to those gathered around. But William maneuvered Lucinda to the side of the blockhouse and led her across the meadow to the multicolored tree line at its edge.

Finally, he removed his hand from her back to stroll alongside her contentedly. The day had turned out exceptionally warm for November, and a pleasant breeze tugged at a few stray strands of Lucinda's hair. The bright sun touched her crown and enhanced the magnificent golden-red color of the tresses she wore pinned neatly at the back of her neck. William had never seen anything like it, or her.

"I hope ye were not waitin' long." Lucinda's melodic voice broke the silence. "I did not mean to sleep so long." A captivating pink blush tinted her freckled cheeks.

When he realized he had become distracted and had not replied promptly, William cleared his throat. "Oh. Uh. No." He rubbed the back of his neck. *Just get to the point.* "I just came to see if you had made a decision whether or not you would continue west." *With me.*

Lucinda's smile was tentative but filled with an infectious joy that warmed his insides. "I would like to go west, if yer offer still stands."

"Of course," William replied with a smile, but then he sobered. "I may not be much of a man, Lucinda, but I always keep my word."

Lucinda gave him a thoughtful look but said nothing at first. "Thank ye for that," she finally offered with a closed-mouth grin. As they continued, she closed her eyes and tilted her chin up to the sun. Contentment shone over every inch of her face as she rubbed her pale fingers over her arms as if to encourage the warmth deeper into her body. Fallen leaves crunched under their feet. William glanced up at the clear blue sky, marked only by a few fluffy clouds. They would certainly be smart to enjoy this odd turn of temperature because winter would likely be full upon them soon. Then it would require all his skill to deliver Lucinda and those in his care safely to their destination.

∼

*B*y the time she and William turned back toward the blockhouse, nearly all the stiffness had worked out of Lucinda's joints. She relished the feel of the warm sun against her face and seeping through her body. The change in weather had been a wonderful surprise when she and William stepped outside, one her body was thoroughly grateful for. After a full night's rest and a stroll in the sunshine, Lucinda almost felt like a new woman. Of course, the endless possibilities that lay before her could give a person fresh energy as well. She smiled as she took in the bright, vibrant colors of the changing leaves that lined the valley and blanketed the mountains beyond. *Thank ye, Lord.*

Lucinda glanced up at William, who had remained silent since she had agreed to continue westward. A small grin played at her lips as she took in his profile. He truly was handsome, even if not conventionally so. But his jawline was strong, his skin tan, and his thick sandy-brown hair almost tempted a woman to reach up and weave her hand right into it. Lucinda swallowed and glanced away, glad for the distraction as they neared the encampments.

At the sight of people, she drifted closer to William, her shoulder brushing his arm before she realized what she had done. His gaze met hers briefly, but he did not move away, as if he knew she needed the solace of his presence. Lucinda tried to keep her head high as they walked, instead of on the dry, crunchy grass at their feet, but her insides quaked.

People peered up at them from where they sat tending to their family or the midday meal. A small child with chubby cheeks toddled up to Lucinda. She smiled and ruffled his shaggy blond hair, but his mother quickly snatched him away. Her dark, piercing look of disdain reminded Lucinda of her father. She glanced away as pain squeezed her heart, but at the gentle warmth of William's hand at the small of her back, she continued on.

Mutters followed them from a gaggle of bachelors gathered around the dying embers of a campfire. She glanced their direction just long enough to discover that their gazes were pointed in her and William's direction. She could not hear their words. Probably a blessing. For surely, she and her lopsided gait were not the topic of conversation.

As they neared the door, one man would not allow such hopeful thoughts. He stood and blocked their path as William tried to return her safely indoors. The man spat a dark-brown substance in her direction, barely missing her skirt and causing William to tuck her close into his side.

The lanky fellow with a scraggly gray beard leered. "Why don't ye get that heathen outa here?"

Beside her, William braced. When he spoke, his voice came out tight, if still polite. "We will head right on inside, sir, if you do not care to step aside."

The man let out a haunting laugh that caused Lucinda to take a step backward. She stopped when her body pressed against William's hard arm, which was still protectively circled around her.

"She is of no threat to you, sir." This time, William's voice was raised. All those in the camps closest to them would hear his words.

The man stepped closer to William and peered at him through narrowed eyes. "And what is it to ye? Is she your little—"

The pest did not get to finish his words. Within seconds, William held him up against the wall of the blockhouse, a large hand around his thin neck and his feet dangling below him.

Lucinda's eyes widened, and William's voice became a bellow, loud enough for everyone to hear now. "I will kindly insist that you do not lay vile insinuations against this woman. She is twice the human being you could ever dream of being. And should you wish to survive this journey west, it would be in your best interest not to become my enemy. Because I will be one of the only things standing between you and sure death."

The skinny man's hands went in the air, and his eyes rounded. "I...I did not mean no harm," he whined.

William dropped the man to the ground and let him cower in a crumpled heap.

Meanwhile, Lucina's heart hammered against the inside of her chest. Her ears pounded with each rapid pump of blood, and her lungs seemed to have stopped their intake of air. Without waiting for William, she rushed ahead into the blockhouse. Inside, tears streamed down her face as she gasped for air. What had she been thinking to believe that things could be different for her? That the general populous could accept her?

Within seconds, William was by her side. Rebecca's concerned murmur barely reached her ears, and William's deep voice replied with more low words she could not make out. Lucinda did not attempt to interpret their conversation, though. Instead, she squeezed her eyes shut and dug her nails into the wooden chair-back as she gripped it. When she felt William's hand at her elbow, she spun to face him. "I cannae go with ye," she sobbed as she shook her head emphatically.

William's grip tightened on her elbow, and he took a step closer. The sobs wracking her chest slowed as she stared into his hazel eyes. "Of course you can," he urged. Such an honest plea filled both his voice and gaze that it caused her tears to surge once more.

"I cannae see ye hurt on my account. I cannae see

anyone hurt on my account! It is not worth it. My father was right." The last realization broke Lucinda's heart to the point that when William stepped close to her, she crumbled into his chest. Without a thought to propriety, she pressed into the solid wall that was his body, seeking the strength and comfort his embrace offered.

William wrapped one arm tightly around her slender form and used the other to tuck a gloved hand under her chin and lift her gaze to his face. "It is worth it. *You* are worth it. I will do whatever it takes to keep you safe."

Lucinda's brow puckered as she stared up at William. A question formed on her lips but was interrupted by Rebecca, who suddenly appeared with a cup of warm tea.

With her arrival, William stepped away, putting a couple of feet between them.

Rebecca handed over the deep-amber liquid, one of her dark brows raised as she looked at Lucinda. "Do not forget our discussion last night. It does not matter what people think of ye. God's opinion is the only one that matters."

Lucinda frowned and glanced between the two people before her. How did they have so much faith in her? More than anything, she wanted to believe the words they spoke. She wanted to believe that somewhere out there, God had created a place just for her. And desperately, she wanted to believe that she deserved a full life, just as much as the next person. But worry took root deep inside her and wound its anxious fingers throughout her body. Fear accompanied it, squeezing her heart in a vice grip and reminding her that she was nothing.

Rebecca seemed to sense her hesitation. "Ye can stay

right inside here with me until ye leave. Then ye will be ridin' with William, an' he will protect ye. On the trail, he will be one of the only guides, so people will respect him in a way they might not here. They will have to if they want to live." She glanced at William, who gave a grim nod.

"There is nothing easy about the journey we are about to embark on. People will die, even if you stay here."

The breath left Lucinda's body. Why had she not considered the dangers that lay ahead? Suddenly, she was not thinking about herself or the problems her presence would pose. Her gaze locked onto William's face and roamed over his body. Not even three days had passed since their meeting, but he had already provided a comfort and companionship like none she had ever known. Not to mention the fact that he had risked his life for her when she had been a perfect stranger. How could she send him out into the wilderness without her and risk never seeing him again?

"I will go." The words were out of her mouth before she knew it. And they carried a strength with them that did not align with what she felt inside. As William gave her a slow, determined nod, she sent up a silent prayer. *Please let me have made the right decision, Lord.*

CHAPTER 6

*J*oints stiff and sore from sleeping on the hard ground, Lucinda stood and stretched her arms high in the air as she took in the tall peaks before them, bathed in the early-morning sunlight. The Clinch Mountains stood proudly waiting for them to pass through the narrow gap at their base on what was their second day of travel. Every shade from gold to crimson blanketed their surfaces, intermixed with the deep greens of pine and cedar. At their tops, a thin layer of white snow provided a reminder to the travelers in the meadow below that seasonal temperatures had returned. Cold air nipped at Lucinda's nose and cheeks as her breath formed a plume of white in front of her face. She wrapped her arms around herself as a chill swept through her body and caused a quick, involuntary shiver.

"Cold?" A deep voice sounded behind her.

A smile crept over Lucinda's lips before she turned to greet William. She had already become accustomed to the baritone sound that covered her with the comfort of a warm blanket.

"Nay. Just a wee chill, thanks be to Mary 'n' Rebecca." She shrugged her right shoulder, covered in the dark wool coat Mary had given her at the beginning of their journey.

"Good." William nodded, but his mouth pulled into a thin line.

Without thinking, Lucinda stepped closer. "What it is?"

"I want you to stick right by my side today. And do exactly what I say. No matter what."

Lucinda's brows furrowed. "Of course," she replied, but she regarded him carefully. His expression appeared as serious as he sounded. And even now, with her agreement, a muscle in his tightly clenched jaw twitched. "Is something wrong?"

William cleared his throat as his golden-brown eyes bore into her. A tingle of apprehension ran up the back of Lucinda's neck. Finally, he flicked his gaze to where the rest of the travel party was packing up camp before he moved even nearer to her. A protective hand wound around her arm while he placed himself between her and the others. He leaned close to her ear as he spoke, causing her heart to speed at his nearness. "There are Cherokee and Shawnee that still believe we should not intrude upon their lands. Moccasin Gap is a common place for their ambushes. It is only a narrow pass with high ground on either side, providing perfect vantage points and easy cover for those who oppose westward expansion."

Lucinda nodded. "I will stay close," she confirmed quietly. When she turned to look up into William's face, mere inches from hers, his eyes had taken on a haunted look. Her stomach twisted, but before she could do or say anything, he relinquished his grip on her arm and turned on his heel. Lucinda nibbled on her lower lip as she watched him stalk back over to Mr. Robertson and a man they referred to as Donegal.

Then she turned her gaze back toward the waiting peaks. Her heart ached as she considered those who had lived so peacefully on the land they were about to enter before newcomers intruded. Was it right for them to continue on? To take someone else's land as their own? But what option did she have? As soon as she stepped foot outside her father's cabin, she no longer had a home. And what of the others in their travel party? Were they facing their own injustices? Was this their only hope for freedom as well?

God, please grant us safe travel. Please guide us to a land where we can live peaceably.

~

*U*nease gnawed at William's insides as his body moved with the rhythmic gait of his horse. His gaze darted from the mountain rising up on their right to the one on their left, but nothing seemed amiss among the vibrantly colored trees and forest floor strewn with drying leaves. He strained for the sounds of Lucinda's gelding behind him, but he could not seem to hear anything over the pounding of his own heart. No matter how many times he passed through Moccasin Gap, it never became easier. Especially since last winter's hunting trip.

The terror-filled cries still haunted William in the quiet of dark. On that fateful night, the sound had carried through the valley to where he camped alone and woken him from a deep sleep. He had stayed hidden in the small cave, wide awake, until dawn, as he waited to see if he would become the next victim.

As unbidden images of scalped bodies slipped through his mind, bile rose up the back of his throat. William swallowed both the taste and the memories. He could not let that happen to Lucinda.

His horse's pale golden head jerked up and her nostrils flared, causing William's pulse to jump. The whites of the mare's eyes shone as she tilted her head to the left and began to prance in place. William refrained from the soft murmurs he would normally use to calm his horse as he scanned the hillside. No movement flashed in his field of vision, but an eerie silence filled his ears.

Suddenly, a rustle of leaves on the forest floor to his right sent his mare skittering sideways. Instinctively, William swung his rifle around and had it to his shoulder before he spied the source of the sound. His shoulders and the barrel of his gun both sagged at the sight of a gray squirrel bounding through dead leaves toward a large oak. Its bushy tail swished as it scurried up the tree trunk, accompanied by the violent barking of a dog from the rear of the party.

A shout from the same direction captured his attention next, but a quick glance verified it was only a reprimand for the dog. A gush of air left William's body before he met Lucinda's gaze. His brow lowered when, instead of amusement, he found her face drawn with fear and concern. Though the trail was narrow, barely wide enough for the two horses, he sidled over next to her where he could feel the comfort of her leg against his. Her gray-blue eyes stared up at him expectantly, and he tried to work up the words to tell her all was well, but they would not come. Instead, he allowed his gaze to roam over each mountainside once before he let out a low, rumbling whisper. "Let us get out of here."

Without waiting for her nod, he asked his horse to pick up a trot. Robertson and Donegal watched from several lengths ahead on the trail. William met Robertson's sharp gaze, and the man immediately turned and followed suit. They could not afford not to. While it was dangerous to hurry along the uneven trail littered with roots and branches, it was more dangerous to linger within that dreadful pass.

~

*L*ucinda kicked her right foot out of the stirrup and stretched it out, making a small circular motion without touching her horse. She withheld a groan as she worked the pained joint, her gaze turning to the heavy clouds which had gathered overhead as the day progressed. Every sign, including the drop in temperature, bespoke of the coming snow. As much as she wished to ride up alongside William and inquire as to when they would make camp, she held her tongue and her place within the procession. Though the sun threatened to dip down over the horizon within the hour, Lucinda placed her trust in the leadership of the guides. Namely, the one that turned to glance in her direction ever so often.

In an attempt to ignore her pained, weary body, she turned her attention to the steady gurgle of water over rocks on their right. They followed Troublesome Creek to the point where they would cross the Clinch River. But William sent another glance her way, and when his gaze lingered this time, she flicked her eyes to his face. Her own brows drew together as she took in his furrowed brow and drawn mouth. She watched him in the hope he would see the concern in her eyes, but after a moment, he turned his attention back to the trail ahead. Lucinda frowned.

However, her curiosity was settled several minutes later when the men ahead of her stopped. As she halted her tall bay next to William's palomino, something clinched deep within her. They had reached the Clinch River, and its wide, smooth surface and murky water loomed before them like an impassable fortress.

With wide eyes, Lucinda turned to William. His mare stepped closer as his gaze met hers, his jaw set. "It is not as bad as it looks. This is the easiest place to cross, and we have had a dry spell." His Adam's apple bobbed as he swallowed. "I will make sure you make it safely across."

William's voice was determined, and Lucinda gave him a nod. But as she gauged the distance across the water before them, she wondered if only the hand of God would be able to see her across. Surely, they were not the first to cross the expanse of water. Still, worry tugged her mouth into a frown.

As the men dismounted and conversed, Lucinda slipped from her horse, holding back a grimace as her aching ankles bore the impact of her weight. Thankfully, within minutes, William was by her side. His broad shoulders and reassuring presence helped ease the tension coiling in her stomach. She searched his hazel gaze as he approached, her own brows raised expectantly.

"Robertson and I will go first. We will carry ropes so that we can help guide your horse across next. Donegal will stay behind and help the others cross." William glanced across the river as he spoke, then turned his attention back to her face. His jaw worked as he considered her. "Do you know how to swim?"

Lucinda shook her head as tears sprang into her eyes.

Something flashed in William's gaze. He nodded. "It will be all right. You just have to hang onto your horse."

Lucinda returned his nod. *Lord, please see me through.*

Minutes later, she stood on the bank clinging to her horse's reins as William and Mr. Robertson forded the river, dragging ropes behind that were attached to both their saddles and her horse's bridle. Her heart lurched when they reached the deepest portion and their bodies dipped into the water as their horses began to swim. But their steady progress did not waver, and the two men continued stoically on.

Still, Lucinda's eyes did not leave William's back until he was safely across and his mount had climbed fully onto the far shore, which was littered with small, pale rocks nearly the same shade of tan as his horse. He and

Robertson dumped the water out of their shoes and stomped on the ground, even flinging their arms to dispel as much water as possible. Lucinda could not imagine how cold they were. Although she would soon find out. She shivered at the thought, eyeing the glassy surface warily.

William motioned for her to cross. With a deep breath, she placed her left foot in the stirrup and swung up onto her bay gelding. She clucked to her horse and asked him to step into the chilly river. Her heart skittered in her chest as the water slowly rose around her horse's legs.

Within seconds, her feet and ankles had slipped into its icy depths. She sucked in a breath as the freezing liquid continued up her body. A scream threatened to erupt from her mouth, but she held it in. That was, until her entire torso suddenly dipped under. Her horse seemed to fall from beneath her as his feet left the ground and he began to swim. The frigid water stole her breath and wrapped its tendrils up her throat, threatening to suffo-cate her before she even slipped under. With her feet coming loose from her stirrups, her skirts bogged her down. Her horse's steady clip pulled it farther away from her, out of her grasp. Desperately, her hand sliced back and forth through the water in search of something she could hold onto. Terror gripped her when nothing met her touch and her sinking body was forced to take one last breath.

*W*illiam's heart dropped to the pit of his stomach. Even from the shore, he could see the fear and desperation that filled her eyes as her horse swam away. "Do not let go of the reins," he bellowed right before her head dipped underwater, leaving only her hat in her wake. The chill that sliced through William's body had nothing to do with the freezing air. Without a thought, he leapt into action. He thew off his leather coat and boots, the rope connecting him to her mount dropping to the ground. Then he ran straight into the water.

"Lucinda," William called before the icy depths claimed him once more.

Her head crested briefly. "Wil—" She gasped, and her arms slapped furiously at the water. Her skirts had to weigh her down.

William swam as quickly as he could toward her splashing——near the dangerous current that could claim even the most experienced swimmers. His heart pounded and his fingers grew numb.

When an eerie silence fell upon his ears, William froze. He glanced up, and his heart skipped a beat. Only a ripple in the water remained where Lucinda had struggled. *No.* He forced his body forward faster, his arms and lungs burning in protest. He reached for her but found nothing. Panic gripped him. "Lucinda!" His call was met only by the sound of his pounding heart and ragged breath.

Taking in a large gulp of air, he dunked his head underwater and glanced around the murky depths. *There.*

Though her eyes were closed and her mouth open as bubbles escaped, her hand reached up toward him as if she knew he was there. Meanwhile, her body slipped lower and lower. William dived. Then with a force he did not know he possessed, William kept them both afloat as he hauled her to the surface.

He tucked her slender body tightly against his with one arm and used the other to draw them toward the shore. Unease twisted his insides when she remained silent. The swim back seemed to take forever, but once his feet were firmly planted on the bank, William lifted Lucinda up into his arms, soaked skirts and all. As he carried her across the rock-strewn sand bar to the edge of the tree line, she started to cough and sputter. He did not even care that the first of the spray splattered his face before she was able to consciously turn away. His own body could finally breathe again, knowing that she was not gone from him.

Carefully, William knelt with her upper body across his lap. In the background, Robertson's instructions to the party drifted to him. But William did not hear the words. His only focus was Lucinda.

He searched her pale face as she leaned over to cough up more of the water that had threatened to drown her. Her fingers bit into the flesh of his arms through his water-logged shirt, but he barely felt the sting. Instead, he kept her wrapped in his arms and he waited for her retching to subside, his own heart in his throat.

When Lucinda finally stilled, he eased her torso to the ground but kept his hands on her thin arms. Her skin had lost its warm creaminess, and her lips were turning blue.

She closed her eyes and her body started to shiver violently. William turned to see who was available to assist. "Carter," he barked the name he thought belonged to the young blonde who had just swam across the river. "Come with me. We have to make camp."

William glanced down at Lucinda as he lifted her into his arms once more. Her chest rose and fell with long, full breaths. Still, the tension in William's chest did not ease.

Slowly, her eyelids fluttered open to reveal her eyes, which had faded to a pale, exhausted gray. One corner of her mouth tried to lift in a smile despite her teeth chattering. "Th-thank ye...f-for s-saving me."

William's heart clenched as he strode into the darkening forest in search of a safe site to make camp for the night. He had to start a fire and warm Lucinda.

CHAPTER 7

*L*ucinda pulled her heavy eyelids open, but her eyes met with little more than darkness. Firelight flickered and danced across the colorful leaves overhead, behind which peeked a deep black sky. Slowly, she became aware of other sensations. Though her joints ached, she did not rest on hard earth or even a simple pallet of furs. Instead, beneath the fur seemed to be a thick, fluffy surface with harder lines intermixed. The scent of pine wafted to her nose, along with the smell of burning wood. And though her clothes still felt damp to her touch, they were warm. Her brows came together as she lifted a hand to explore her surroundings. She was nestled in a thick, heavy cocoon of furs. In fact, furs were even rolled and placed on each side of her head.

Perplexed, Lucinda attempted to sit up.

"Whoa," came William's deep voice from next to her, and a hand pressed against her shoulder. Then his face was above hers, and for what seemed like the first time since they had met, a smile tugged at his mouth. Her insides flip-flopped at the handsome sight, and she had to fight down her own grin. "You are awake."

Lucinda nodded, fur tickling the side of her face. "Did everyone make it across all right?" Her voice came out in a hoarse rasp, and her throat felt as if sand grated against it.

William's face disappeared from her field of vision for a moment. No answer came to her question. A bad sign? Her mouth twisted.

"Here, you need to take some of this broth." William moved in close enough that he could hold her head with one hand and lift the spoon to her mouth with the other.

Lucinda accepted the sip and allowed the warm liquid to soothe her insides. Then she attempted to rise again. William cleared his throat and gave her a sharp look. "I can do it meself," she protested.

He shook his head and lifted another spoonful. "You need the rest."

Lucinda closed her eyes as she savored the broth. Then she flicked her gaze back to William's face. In the shadow of the firelight, one could barely tell pock marks marred his skin. His profile was so strong and reassuring. And the feel of his thick hand at the back of her neck, free of his gloves for once... The touch warmed her more than the broth. If there was anyone she could see spending the rest of her days with, it was this man. But that was not an option for her, and she would be on her own again as soon as they reached their destination. So Lucinda gave the handsome man fussing over her a pointed look.

"Is anyone else resting?"

William's face turned wry. "Well, yes, everyone but the

watch. It is the middle of the night. And besides, not everyone almost drowned." He raised his eyebrows at her.

She pursed her lips. "Did anyone else?" She asked the question slowly and plainly.

"Almost drown?" William tried to avoid the question again, but the sadness in his gaze gave away the answer.

"How many?" Lucinda searched his eyes. It was all she could do not to reach out to him, to try to ease the pain hidden within their hazel depths.

"Just one." His answer came softly and revealed that to him, one was too many.

Lucinda's heart squeezed for the person's family. She tamped down the urge to press William and find out who. But this time, she did reach over and place her hand on the thick leather that covered his knee.

Fire flared in his gaze.

"Have ye rested?"

The muscle in his jaw ticked. Breathing seemed to become difficult as he met her gaze with an intensity that warmed her insides. Respect and admiration welled within her. Not only had William saved her from the depths of the river, but his lack of response now also told that he had stayed up half the night watching over her. Lucinda's brow wrinkled. *Why?*

She was nothing, no one. Only a burden. She certainly did not deserve this kind of attention. And yet, William seemed determined to protect her with his life.

~

A soft giggle next to William drew his attention. Without realizing, he had fallen back beside Lucinda as the trail widened. And now she grinned over at him, joy radiating from her face. She motioned toward the sky and the tiny white flakes that had started to fall with her slender, gloved hand. "It is snowin'."

To his surprise, a deep chuckle rumbled from his own chest. "It is."

When he had spotted the first flake, William had stifled a groan. To him, the turn in weather signaled a difficult journey ahead. And yet Lucinda stared at the sky in a state of wonder, completely mesmerized by the frozen precipitation that landed on her shoulders and quickly melted into her dark wool coat. William frowned as he made a mental note to ensure she stayed warm after the events of the day before. His insides clenched at the thought of losing her to pneumonia or some other cold-weather disease.

William forced his attention back to his surroundings. He had to get a grip on himself and the barrage of emotions this woman stirred within him. But as he glanced at the landscape around them, all sense was lost. Instead, his mind was filled with the vision of another one of those wondrous smiles and the joy that would gleam in Lucinda's eyes as she encountered another miracle she had never seen before. William was hopeless to resist the temptation of such a sight.

"Follow me," he instructed as he guided his mare off the trail. He motioned an arm for the leg of the travel party behind them to continue on. Then he dismounted and waited for Lucinda to do the same. She glanced over at him expectantly, and he had to school his expression to remain blank. "Careful on this rock," William advised. "It will be slick, especially for the horses."

After a few steps, the horses' hooves clattered onto the smooth stone surface leading toward a large rock structure. As they neared, the seemingly solid structure opened up to reveal a great natural tunnel with a view of the snowy woods on the other side. Lucinda gasped and glanced in his direction, a smile stretching across her face. But she continued to walk silently next to him until they stepped up into the tunnel itself, where the stone ceiling stopped the snow and the click of hooves echoed off the walls.

William took Lucinda's reins so that she could step back and admire the natural tunnel. She turned in a circle and took in every inch of the magnificent structure. Then she turned her look of awe upon him. "This is incredible," she breathed as she came back to stand in front of him. Her eyes appeared misted, but her smile still stretched wide across her face. "I have never seen anything like it."

Her revelation made his heart ache. Suddenly, a deep desire to show Lucinda the world surged within William. This beautiful woman had never been provided the opportunity to see the world outside the four walls of her father's cabin. Guilt gnawed at William's stomach. How much had he underappreciated his surroundings over the past four years, consumed by the pain and guilt of his sister's passing? William stepped closer to Lucinda, to the comfort he felt in her presence.

Her freckled cheeks were flushed pink from the cold,

her mouth slightly parted. And those captivating eyes. They did not look upon him with shame or pity. There was no hate or disapproval within their depths. No, Lucinda looked up at him with admiration and acceptance. His breaths became ragged. Without thinking about what he was doing, he slipped a hand around her waist and pulled her close. More than anything, he wanted to become lost in her gaze and never leave. Because for the first time in four years, he felt good and worthy. Not like a despicable human being who did not even deserve the breath in his lungs.

"William?" She breathed his name, bringing his gaze down to her pink lips. Her voice was tentative but carried a question. A question he longed to answer.

A shiver ran down his spine and pressed him closer to her. Her slender body curved perfectly into his, her small hands curled at his chest. He closed his eyes and absorbed the sweet feeling. How good it felt to hold someone who believed in him.

Without realizing, he had allowed his face to nestle against hers. He wanted so desperately to close the gap, to cover her mouth with his and lean into the image she held of him. To strive to be that man. But he could not. In a final moment of strength, he pulled back and cleared his throat. "We should probably get back to the group." Turning his horse, he handed over her reins.

Lucinda nodded but did not say a word.

*B*y the time they rode into camp, Lucinda could focus on little other than the weather and her own misery. Thoughts of William and their morning encounter had filled much of the day, countless thoughts swirling around her mind much like those first fluffy snowflakes that had blown about on the wind.

But now, every inch of her tense body ached, and her hands and feet had long since gone numb. Snow and ice pelted them relentlessly. The gusting wind blew it up under the hood of the fur cloak William had fashioned for her. The precious gift he had presented to her before they picked up travel again after a short midday respite had generated within her a deep gratitude. Because what had begun as a beautiful, peaceful snowfall had quickly turned menacing as the temperature dropped and the precipitation came heavier. Travel that afternoon had been slow and grueling, with low visibility. At times, she could barely make out the rump of William's mount in front of her.

Lucinda had steeled herself with the fact that she was better clothed than most of the travel party. And despite her condition, which pained her joints further and further with each drop in temperature, she had no right to complain. Many in the travel party bore tattered coats and no gloves. So, after she slowly and carefully dismounted from her horse, she hobbled him near William's mount and immediately set to helping gather firewood.

With a thick layer of hard, wet snow coating the wintery world around them, the task proved difficult. However, she did emerge from the thick cover of a tall pine with a few logs which would suffice. As she slipped from the branches, Lucinda spied a family with several young children huddled around a hopelessly small flame. Her footsteps crunched over the frozen snow as she approached the dark-haired woman who shook violently, having shed her own coat to cover two of her toddlers. But as Lucinda drew near, the woman's deep-brown eyes flashed, and she bolted to her feet.

Lucinda hesitated. "Just some wood, to keep the bairns warm." She lifted the small logs, then nodded toward the shivering children. She winced inwardly as her mother's term for babes slipped out.

The woman's chest puffed out, and she crossed her arms. "My *children* do not need any wood from the likes of you."

Lucinda glanced from her angry face to the tiny ones peeking out from the coat. Then she took a step backward. She almost jumped when a hand at her back stayed her.

"Is there a problem here?" Reverend Donaldson appeared at her side. Both women turned their gazes upon his clean-shaven face.

All was quiet for a moment before the other woman spoke up. "No, Reverend. She was simply offering us some wood." Conveniently, her husband showed up at that moment, his own arms miraculously laden with wood. Would it be dry enough to burn? But Lucinda kept her mouth shut. The woman lifted her chin. "But as you can see, we have plenty."

"Yes," Reverend Donaldson replied tightly. "What a blessing."

As she and the Reverend turned away from the foul-tempered woman, Lucinda had to swallow back a smile at the double meaning of those final words. She had quickly learned that while he delivered fiery sermons, Reverend Donaldson was quite an amiable person. And though they'd had little interaction, he never treated her differently than the others in the travel party. As now, he escorted her toward where William, Donegal, and a couple of others were making camp. He walked slowly to stay at her side as she limped forward.

After they were several yards from the woman and her family, he cleared his throat and spoke only loud enough to be heard above the surrounding sounds. "Lucinda, I wonder if you understand what I mean when I refer to a woman's virtue."

Lucinda's gaze snapped up to his face, which he kept trained forward. Then she glanced at the ground as heat crept up her neck. Though she knew little, she was aware that there were things she had yet to learn of what occurred between a man and woman under the sanctity of marriage. "Yes, sir," she replied meekly.

"Good. Then I feel compelled to remind you that perceived virtue can often hold the same weight as true virtue."

Though there was no scolding in his light tone, Lucinda's eyes widened. Understanding rippled through her, and she fought the temptation to glance back toward the angry woman. "Aye, Reverend. I understand."

"Good." He gave her a smile as he turned toward her, his light-blue eyes crinkling at the corners. "I have spoken with Mr. Cole as well." Then, without further explanation, he left the weight of his words hanging behind him.

William was placing a fur over a rough bed of pine boughs. He glanced up at her. "Your pallet is ready."

She nodded, but her heart was in her throat as she watched him move away. They had been alone together. What would the others think? And what would William himself think? She had not meant to trap him. Cold tears filled the rims of her eyes, but she blinked them back and went to begin supper.

CHAPTER 8

*T*he next morning dawned bright and cold. But William's brain felt as muddled as the earth below them, which had turned into a mash of melting snow and soft dirt. No matter how he attempted to focus on the slowly rising terrain, his mind kept wandering back to Reverend Donaldson's words regarding Lucinda's virtue. His stomach twisted as his palomino mare took one steady step after another. *How could I have been so foolish?* Especially that moment he had drawn Lucinda away from the others. He had only meant to nurture the joy that shone in her face at the coming of the first snow. But he had forgotten the implications of spending unchaperoned time with a woman. And now she would be tied to him against her will. The thought made his insides roil with guilt. No woman deserved such a fate.

William was whisked from his thoughts when his horse froze on the trail. Her light-golden skin rippled across her shoulder. William's pulse picked up as he glanced around, checking for danger. All seemed well, but his gaze landed on Lucinda where she rode several feet behind him. Her horse had developed a limp and moved slowly over the boggy terrain. He patiently waited for her to draw alongside him and halt.

"I am sorry, William." She shook her head. "He stepped on a rock. I did not see it until it was already too late." Her mouth pinched and her forehead wrinkled. The concern and unwarranted guilt in her stirred something protective within him, and he had to fight the urge to reach out and place his hand on hers. Instead, he swallowed.

"It is all right. The terrain is treacherous today. It will be a blessing if we make it through with only a bruised hoof. But it would be best if you ride with me while I pony him."

Lucinda hesitated, and she shifted her notice to the line of travelers behind them—doubtlessly considering the thoughts of the others. How did he ever pull her into this mess? As he took in her pale, freckled face wrought with indecision, he felt the same longing as before to fix everything for her. To heal her aches. What was it about this woman who snuck so easily beneath his skin?

He cleared his throat. "It will be fine. We will talk later." He lingered in the pool of her gaze for only a moment longer, lest she see too deeply within his soul, then bent to take her horse's reins into hand.

Within moments, she had slid from her bay and mounted his palomino behind him. At first, her thin arms slipped tentatively around his middle. But as the elevation became steeper and temperatures dipped even lower, she held tightly to him and pressed her cheek against his back.

As they inched their way up the steep mountainside, William's mare slipped in the mud and nearly went down. Lucina let out a little cry. Lowering the reins in his hand, he gave the horse her head. Lucinda's fingers, albeit uneven and abnormal, gripped the edge of his leather coat. He swallowed and attempted to focus beyond her warmth to their surroundings.

Behind them, a scream sounded—and chilled William to the bone more than the frigid temperature. He turned in his saddle just in time to see a horse slide backward and crash into the one behind it. His eyes widened, and a whimper came from Lucinda. William quickly transferred both sets of reins into one hand so that he could wrap her small form in his arm and shield her from the view. Both horses and riders tumbled backward over jagged rocks and saplings until they crashed in a tangled heap against a large oak. William closed his eyes and looked away as the men around them hurried over to see if there were survivors.

A small band would have to stay behind to deal with the consequences of the pileup, whatever burials or medical attention were required. But there was no way to set up camp exposed on the mountainside. It was too dangerous, and the scene before them was a cruel reminder of that. William slowly released Lucinda and turned before asking his horse to walk on. He needed to get her off this mountain.

~

*J*f Lucinda thought uphill travel was nerve-wracking, downhill was twice as much so. As William leaned back, she found herself pressed curiously between him and the horse's rump, which made her back sting and sear with pain. She held tightly to William and fought to keep the position. And to remember to breathe. Meanwhile, it felt as if she would slide right off over the horse's neck if William was not in front of her. And she did not wish to consider what would happen if the palomino were to slip or stumble. Images of the disturbing accident that happened coming up the mountain flashed in her mind's eye. William had done his best to protect her from the sight, but it was too late. The image of the mass of mangled bodies, both human and equine, could never be forgotten.

By the time they reached the bottom and stopped to set up camp, Lucinda could hardly move for the pain that had settled into her spine. She bit back tears as she carefully slid to the ground and stretched.

William followed and moved closer to her. Even under the shadow of his hat, concern was written in the lines on his face. "You are in pain."

Lucinda attempted to force a weak smile onto her face. "I am fine." The words came out squeezed and hoarse. Strained and forced.

William's mouth settled into a thin line. "No. You need to rest. I will make your pallet, and you are to lie down."

A small smile tugged at her mouth. She placed a

gloved hand on his arm and shook her head. "I have to keep movin'."

The muscle in William's jaw worked as he considered her words. "Fine," he conceded, though he hesitated before he turned and walked away.

Cold wrapped around her that very moment. The chill and breathtaking pain were reminders of the concerns that had plagued her all morning. As she forced her body to move, her mind swirled with what William would say regarding her tainted virtue. Would he want to marry her? Should she even let him?

~

*A*s soon as she was able, Lucinda tucked herself under her furs for the night and prayed for the pain in her back to ease. Despite her discomfort, exhaustion claimed her quickly.

Lucinda jerked awake at the sound of her name near her ear. She bolted upright, expecting her father's disapproving glare. Instead, William's pleasant profile greeted her, merely inches from her face, illuminated by the campfire that flickered beside them. How long had she slumbered?

His Adam's apple bobbed as he swallowed. "We need to talk."

Lucinda frowned and nodded, then maneuvered into a cross-legged sitting position. With a glimpse around camp, it was evident that William had waited until everyone but the guards were asleep before he had awakened her. So she kept her furs pulled over her legs as he settled onto the ground next to her. The conflict in his face was clear as she watched him, waiting for what he had to say. The sight tore her to pieces inside. She wanted nothing more than to reach out and comfort him. But the same torment bubbled within herself. Finally, she chose to ease his pain.

"William, I cannae marry ye."

His brows lowered, and his lips pursed. "What do you mean?"

Lucinda met the warm hazel eyes that bore into her, and her heart wrenched in her chest. Why couldn't she be a whole, beautiful woman deserving of this man? "I am broken, William. I cannae offer ye a family. I do not even know if I could carry a child. I would only be a burden to ye. Ye should marry someone who can be all ye deserve an' be a proper helpmate to ye, give ye a beautiful family."

Amazingly, the furrow between his brows only deepened before he shook his head and looked away. "You do not know all there is to know about me. I do not deserve a wife at all. And I do not even know if I can father children either."

Lucinda tilted her head to the right as she took in the pain etched across his expression. A pain she recognized and understood. A deep-seated feeling of unworthiness and disgrace. She moved up onto her knees, drawing closer to the man before her. Then she slipped her hand from her glove, reached out as she had longed to, and placed her fingers on his face. She cringed inwardly at the sight of them but focused on the feel of the prickly stubble along his jaw and the soft, pock-marked skin above. Warmth stirred within her and replaced the chill of the night. Could she be what he needed? A sad frown tugged at her mouth. He deserved so much more than her. But if she married him, could she help him see himself how she saw him? How God saw him? Was this all part of God's plan for her?

"William, I hold ye in the highest regard. An' I do not hesitate to put me life in yer hands..." But was this truly for the best? She had never meant to saddle a man with her burdensome self. He turned his face to her then, and the golden depths of his eyes pulled her in. Behind the pain was an ounce of hope. And she longed to feed that hope. "I will marry ye if ye wish. If ye truly do not mind takin' me as I am."

William's eyes took on a tenderness as they searched her face, and his expression softened. He took her small hand into his larger, gloved one. "You are beautiful exactly as you are." But then he seemed to draw back from her, to shield himself once more. "I will marry you because it is the right thing to do. I was the one that made it seem as if your virtue had been tainted, and I will be the one to take the responsibility. I will not let any harm come to you or your reputation."

Lucinda slipped her hand from his loose grip as she nodded. But inside, her heart sank. It was exactly as she feared. He was marrying her to remedy his mistake. She could only hope and pray that he never saw her as the burden she truly was, as a mistake. But she raised her chin and strengthened her resolve. No matter the reason for their marriage, she would strive to be the best wife she could. Strive to be a help rather than a hindrance. And to show him the love and acceptance he deserved.

"We will be wed of a mornin'," William whispered before he moved to lie down.

CHAPTER 9

"*May* God bless you and your marriage." Reverend Donaldson gave them a brief nod to indicate the conclusion of their simple ceremony, tucked away in a small band of cedars at the edge of camp. Lucinda offered him a smile as he ducked under the low branches to allow the newlyweds a moment to themselves. Then she turned her tentative gaze upon her new husband. *Husband.* Despite the circumstances, the word stirred an unexpected joy within her heart.

But William's expression was reserved and unreadable, his hazel gaze shadowed by his leather hat as he looked down at her. Lucinda took a step closer so that she could stare fully into the face that normally held a comforting strength. But now emotions warred there, and his lips pulled into a thin line. It tore Lucinda apart inside to know that she had caused the turmoil inside. Tears pricked at the backs of her eyes, but she did not allow them to fall. She kept her voice level as she quietly apologized. "I am sorry for this." Then she turned to walk away.

Before she could make it far, William's voice stopped her. "Wait." Lucinda paused. Through her coat, she felt his strong hand wrap around her arm, and she turned toward his touch. When she looked into his face, the storm had been replaced with tenderness. "This is not your fault."

Lucinda's chest constricted. If only she could believe him. But while William had extended the offer to leave the trail and travel party, she had accepted. If she had not, they never would have been in their predicament. "I am still sorry." Her gaze fell even as she offered him a smile that resulted in more of a frown. "I will try not to be a burden to ye."

An exasperated breath left William's body and made her cringe inwardly. His gloved hand came up to cup the side of her face. Though the leather was cool against her skin, the touch provided a warm reassurance. She longed to lean into it, but instead, simply brought her gaze up to his. The depths of his eyes pulled her in as she recognized a tenderness there. "You are not a burden, Lucinda," he whispered. And with every fiber of her being, she wished to believe him. To believe in the tiny ounce of affection that softened his hazel eyes and the strong lines of his face.

She offered him a small smile. "Ye speak kind words, me husband."

Lucinda attempted to look away then, but William stepped closer. Close enough that the world closed down to the two of them and even the cold wind could not seem to slip in. "Because it is the truth."

If he really meant that, nothing could be more valuable. No matter that her new husband did not kiss her. No matter that their marriage might never be one of love. For that, she could be grateful. For it was more than she could have ever experienced confined to a ramshackle cabin with a father who despised her and thought her only a burden.

~

The sky was a thick, heavy gray when Lucinda set out astraddle her recovered bay as Mrs. William Cole. Winter had overtaken fall, with only a few yellow and brown leaves still clinging to the dark branches of the surrounding trees. Meanwhile, the frozen grass beneath them crunched with each step. The air stung inside her nose, and her breath came in white puffs before her face.

Despite the frigid air and her equally cold husband, who rode several feet ahead of her without looking back, a small bulb of hope nestled within her heart. Though William had hardly glanced her way during their marriage vows, she was now a married woman. And not only was she blessed with a kind, honest husband, but she had also been blessed with an opportunity to serve the Lord. For the first time in her life, she had a purpose. As William's wife, she was in a position to show him the love and grace that he deserved. The love and grace that God would wish to be bestowed upon him. It was a calling that both energized and heartened her to push past the pain and cold.

In the ten years spent hidden away in her father's cabin, her sole purpose in life had been to survive each day. Lucinda had never allowed herself to dream beyond the simple existence of tending to herself and her father day in and day out until her last. But now, each day, she would strive to embody all that her Bible said a wife should be.

She sat taller in the saddle as she imagined herself strong and industrious, helpful, and supportive. With the Lord's help, she could be all that and more. And while she did not venture to believe William could ever return her love, her future still seemed brighter.

~

*W*illiam warily eyed the drop-off to their right as his mare carefully lurched up onto a boulder along one of the countless knobs along Wallen's Ridge. His concern was not for himself, but for his wife. *Wife*. The word sounded as bizarre as the situation felt. Never had he dreamed that he would be a married man. In fact, he had run far from the prospect. Yet somehow, it had caught up with him.

Thoughts of the fair-skinned woman who rode behind him proved dangerously distracting as they followed the ridgeline. Without looking back, William could picture her face. Her fur-lined hood would be pulled over her strawberry-blond hair to guard against the relentless wind that whipped at them, the barren-branched trees providing little windbreak. And though that same hair was pulled back into a tight knot, tiny wisps would dance about her face no matter how she tried to contain them. Tan freckles spread over her nose and cheeks above a pale-pink mouth pulled into a thin line. Despite her best attempts to hide her discomfort, she was in a great deal of pain. A pain that tugged at his insides and he thoroughly wished he had the power to heal. *Only God can do that.*

William frowned and shook the thought from his mind. Then, as soon as the trail flattened and widened enough, he dropped back beside Lucinda. Their marriage may be a tentative one, born out of necessity, but he would still do all in his power to protect the woman in his care.

She looked at him expectantly.

"I believe we should dismount and lead our horses." If only he could feel the same hope that shone from her eyes. Light. Possibility. William forced his thoughts to focus and continued. "The trail is practically nonexistent in places, and these drop-offs along the ridge are dangerous."

Lucinda timidly glanced ahead, where Robertson and Donegal remained astride their mounts. But she did not speak a word of her hesitancy. She simply gave William a small nod and slipped from her mount. William followed suit, for the sake of her pride. He stepped around and took her hand as he spoke urgently. "If your horse falls, let it go. Your life is not worth it."

Lucinda's eyes remained trained on his as she nodded. A small, slow movement. He did his best to ignore the heat that suddenly warmed him from within. He should not stand so close to her. He could not afford to fall in love with her. Guilt swirled in his stomach at the hint of admiration that shone on her face, in the slight upward curve of her lips. He did not deserve it. He stepped away and with one last backward glance, moved ahead.

To his relief, the trail moved away from the ridge for a bit, weaving through the tall, slender, barren trees on relatively level ground. It gave William's nerves a reprieve and released the invisible pressure on his chest. Still, he carefully scanned the area for trouble. Since the sun had peeked out from behind the sky's curtain of clouds, wild animals might venture out into the mild afternoon. His stomach growled and reminded him that with the mountain crossing, they had been unable to stop for a midday respite. His thoughts turned to Lucinda, and his worry returned. Would she be fine without a stop for hydration and nourishment? Should they break before they continued on to the next ridge?

Crack! The unmistakable sound of a tree branch crashing over other branches as it fell to the earth. The hair on the back of William's neck stood up, and his heart plummeted. The sound was too close, as if it were right behind him. Eyes wide, he spun around.

It was as if the scene unfolded before him in slow motion—yet he could not react in time. The dead, rotting tree branch crashed into another limb on its way to the ground, breaking it in half with another crack. The two pieces spiraled downward, and Lucinda's horse careened back, the whites of his eyes showing. Her own eyes turned into wide saucers as her right arm was jerked to its full length before the reins ripped from her fingers. The horse tore free and skittered away. Half of the branch came crashing down over Lucinda. William lunged forward, forgetting his own mount, at the same time she hunkered.

But the limb crashed over her shoulder and right arm, causing her to cry out in pain, before it rolled to the earth in front of her. She sank into a squatted position, her eyes closed. William ran and crouched beside her.

As he scanned for injury, one hand on her back, her eyes snapped open. "I am fine. I am fine," she told him breathlessly and tried to stand.

William stayed by her side as his brows pulled together. "Are you sure? Where did it hit you? Where does it hurt?" He searched her face, her body. He gingerly touched her shoulder where he thought the branch had landed.

Lucinda sucked in her breath as she winced. But then she shook her head and stood, William following suit. "It is nothin'. I am fine."

William's brows crept even lower, and his mouth turned downward. He peered at Lucinda. A tree branch had just fallen on her with enough force to kill a man, but here she stood, insisting she was fine. And no matter how William tried to catch her gaze, she avoided his eye.

"I am fine, William. I need to retrieve me horse." Though there was a bit of strength in her voice, her eyes shone with clear liquid.

"No. Lucinda, I am not worried about your horse. I am worried about you."

Her eyes snapped to his. "Ye are?" She squeaked out the question before a tear slipped down her cheek.

"Of course." William's attention was pulled away by the sound of approaching steps. He instinctively wrapped his left arm around her as he looked up. Donegal approached, William's horse in hand.

"Is all well?" His deep voice carried an accent similar to Lucinda's, and his light-blue eyes shifted between the two of them.

William nodded. "Yes. The party can continue on. We will fall in behind."

Donegal gave a slow, deliberate nod, then turned without a word.

William immediately turned his attention back to Lucinda. "Come here. Let me check you for injury." He looked around as he moved his arm up around her shoulder. She hissed in pain. "Then we will find your horse."

She nodded, her bottom lip tucked under the top as they walked down a gradual embankment. Once they were away from the others, concealed behind a scraggly cedar, William looped his horse's reins over a branch and settled onto the ground beside Lucinda. "I know it is cold, but I need to see your shoulder." He jerked his chin toward her left shoulder, and she gave a timid dip of her head, her eyes wide.

William slowly proceeded to remove her outer layers, his insides twisting at the pain she carefully attempted to conceal as he slipped her arm from her coat sleeve. He hesitated, staring down at the pale skin at the base of her neck. William swallowed. They were a married couple, and there was nothing untoward about checking her shoulder for injury. He shifted so that he was both behind and beside her before he slipped the worn linen fabric from her thin shoulder. Her shoulder bone was pronounced but appeared smooth and intact.

But as he inched the fabric lower, a large red streak had already formed along the top of her shoulder blade.

He gingerly ran a finger over it and watched Lucinda for a reaction that might reveal if anything was broken. Though her lips pressed together and she blinked back tears, she did not flinch.

Before he could react, something else caught his attention. He slipped the fabric a tiny bit lower to reveal the top of a slender scar. Anger bubbled up inside him as he ran a finger over the raised flesh. "Who did this?" His voice came out rougher than he meant, almost a growl.

Lucinda's eyes widened as she gasped, jumped up, and slipped her shirt back into place. She did not meet his gaze. Instead, her arms wrapped around her body and her eyes pressed closed. "It is not...I..."

"William stepped close to her. He slipped an arm around her and brought his other hand up under her chin to coax her gaze to his. "Lucinda, look at me."

When she did, the sight made his heart ache. And finally, everything became clear, including her behavior since the tree branch fell. Fear was written all over her face. The woman was more scared of his reaction, of his scorn, than she was of the pain. His heart might as well have been placed in a vice that had begun to tighten. The revelation lit a fire within that made him wish he had laid her father flat on the ground of that tavern before he had come to her aid. And it renewed the spark he had felt since the day they met, the need to keep her safe at all costs. "It was your father. He did it to you?" He attempted to keep the edge out of his voice, but it was nearly impossible.

Eyes still wide and her bottom lip pinched between her teeth, Lucinda nodded.

William's fingers tightened around her arm, and he had to consciously loosen his grip as he stared into her precious face. How could anyone hurt this beautiful woman? Their own daughter?

Suddenly, William needed his wife to know she never had to fear such torment again. He rubbed her arms before he pulled her close, nestling his hand at the small of her back, where it seemed to meld so perfectly. Her slender body against his provided a comfort he had not experienced in years. As if he might not be so lonely in the world anymore. But he pushed the thought from his mind as he focused solely on reassuring his wife.

"Lucinda, I may never be the husband you deserve. But I will do everything in my power to keep you safe and protected." He ran a tender hand over her shoulder. "And I do not want you ever to feel as if you have to hide your pain from me." With his gaze locked onto hers, he implored her to understand.

She gave another slow nod.

He tipped her chin up. "And I will never do anything to hurt you."

Finally, a small smile graced her soft lips, warming her entire face. And this time, he believed she truly understood when she nodded. He could not help when a grin tugged at the corner of his own mouth. "Good. Now let us see about finding that skittish horse of yours."

*O*nce William and Lucinda caught up to camp, William sent her to warm by the fire while he tended to both of the horses. Lucinda offered him a grin as he took the reins of her bay, still pleased by the promise he had made her on the side of Powell Mountain. She frowned as she shrugged her stiff, sore shoulder but refused to let the added pain diminish her happiness. Ever since William had burst into her life, God had surprised her at each turn. And now she knew that no matter what came of her marriage, she had found someone who accepted her and would serve as her protector. It was more than she could have ever hoped or dreamed.

Her pleasant mood was fed even further when she discovered that Donegal had taken over meal preparation in her absence. As Lucinda settled in next to the warm fire, a tantalizing aroma drifted to her nose. She rubbed her arms as she inhaled deeply. She had only sat there a moment when Donegal's tall, lanky form appeared at her side, carrying a set of tin cups. Without a word, he ladled out a portion and handed it to her.

Lucinda whispered a "thank ye" before she drew the cup up near her face and closed her eyes. The lovely fragrance did as much to warm her as the fire did to thaw her frozen nose. A sigh left her, and she lifted the cup to her mouth. Mm! Donegal must have snuck a few potatoes and onions into his saddlebags before they rode out from Anderson's blockhouse, for the taste that met her lips was hearty and delicious. A pleasant change from what often consisted of only boiled meat. As the warm liquid slid down her throat and warmed her to her toes, she began to daydream about the garden she might plant in the spring.

A smile tugged at the corners of her mouth. Was it truly possible she and William might have a home by spring? Was that too much to dream? Lucinda reined her thoughts in as footsteps approached behind her, alerting her to her husband's presence. She turned to smile up at him, but the gesture died on her lips at the sight of his mouth pulled into a thin line. Her brows lowered in question as he knelt down beside her.

"I have not been able to find a stand of pines to gather branches."

Lucinda tilted her head and offered a gracious grin. "I will be fine with only the furs for the night."

Though he nodded, William seemed unconvinced as he stood and stalked away. How truly blessed she was to be married to such a thoughtful man. *Until he figures out what a burden I am.* The thought assaulted her from the depths of her subconscious, and though she tried to shove it from her mind, it sapped her happiness. No. William was nothing like her father. Even so, the smile slipped from her face, replaced with a sullen frown.

CHAPTER 10

*L*ucinda glanced up from her saddlebag as
William approached. Her stomach sank at his
downcast gaze, his leather hat once again
shielding his face. When his eyes did come up to meet
hers, worry swirled in her middle.

He stepped close. "We have another river crossing
today."

She nipped in a gasp of cool air.

William's gaze softened. His gloved hand came up to
rest on her forearm reassuringly. "I will find a way to keep
you safe."

Lucinda glanced away and nodded. Though William
would do all in his power, he was only one man. *Lord,
please see us safely through.*

"How is your shoulder today?"

Her entire arm—from the top, behind her shoulder
blade, down to her fingertips—ached. Still, she had
stretched it over and over in an attempt to work out some

of the stiffness. But nothing would stop the deep ache that had settled into her joints overnight. It came not from overuse or injury. No, she knew what it meant. The weather would change within the next day or two.

"It is fine." She turned a smile upon her husband.

But William frowned. "Tell me the truth."

Lucinda let out a sigh. "It hurts, but I am fine." She met William's gaze as if to prove her point.

He searched her face before he nodded. "All right." His hand slipped from her arm, and he turned to leave.

"But William?" She took a step in his direction.

"Yeah?" He raised his brow as he turned back.

Lucinda glanced at the mostly clear sky and regretted her decision. But still, she forced the words past her lips. "I dinnae think the weather will hold."

William's brow lowered as he assessed the heavens. When he turned his attention back to her, concern and acceptance settled on his face rather than humor or dismissal. "We cross early in the day. And if all goes well, we should make Martin's Station before nightfall."

Lucinda nodded and offered a weak smile. "That will be good." But as she flexed her stiff, sore fingers, a ripple of unease traveled through her. She pushed the sensation away. She would not give way to fear over the impending river crossing.

~

*L*ucinda gasped as the frigid water of the Powell River rose up to claim her chest and back. From behind, she curled her fingers into the worn fabric of William's shirt.

"I have you," William responded, his voice hoarse and ragged as he gripped her hand.

Lucinda gasped again at the sudden shock of his icy, wet touch. But she grasped his thick, muscular hand as tightly as she could.

As she struggled to coax air into her lungs, her mind was temporarily distracted from the freezing water that swirled around her. Instead, she was lost in the sensation of her hand in her husband's. For the first time, their hands touched skin to skin. He did not shy away from her awkward, uneven fingers. Instead, he clutched her hand with a strength that comforted and reassured, that held tightly as if she were a precious gift. Lucinda had never felt such an embrace.

She was still wrapped in the sensation when the horse below them surged upward as her hooves caught on solid ground. With a great sigh of relief, Lucinda rested her forehead against William's broad back. His hand tightened momentarily around hers in response, which made a smile spread across her face. As they left the water, she soaked in the mild warmth of a ray of sunshine—and the feel of the soft fabric over her husband's hard back against her forehead. Joy bubbled inside her at the oneness she felt with her husband. Even the cold breeze that ruffled her hair and slipped through her shirtsleeves could not dampen her peace. Not only had William seen her through, but he seemed to understand her even without words.

〜

*N*o matter how she tried, Lucinda could not stop the shivering that plagued her body. With every step they had taken toward Martin's Station, the temperature had dropped lower. The air had turned downright frigid and slipped icy tendrils under her hood to claw at her face. Even her bay gelding quaked beneath her. Lucinda hunched in the saddle and wrapped her arms around herself beneath her fur cloak, giving her horse his head. Her only consolation was the knowledge that Martin's Station loomed on the horizon, and each step her horse plodded forward drew her closer. Otherwise, her mind and body were numb. She did not even know how many paces ahead William rode. But she trusted her mount to follow behind.

"Lucinda?" The sound of her name drew her from her frozen stupor. Her brows pulled together as she opened her eyes to the icy air and turned toward the man's voice. *William.* Her heart leapt at the sight of her husband riding along beside her. She blinked and focused past the tears that appeared in her eyes as the frigid wind stung them. Behind William, the open meadow was skirted with barren trees, whose branched creaked under the gusts. Lucinda shuddered. "Martin's Station is right up ahead at the edge of this valley. Donegal rode ahead to alert them of our arrival. Can you make it that far?"

Lucinda nodded her reply before she turned her gaze ahead. While she could make out the dark form of a building, it was still only a tiny blot of darkness in the falling dusk. And still seemed a world away.

She stifled the groan that threatened to erupt from her body when her horse hesitated beneath her. Lucinda stretched her arm out from beneath her fur cloak to rub the cold brown hair covering his shoulder. But she did not turn back to William. She could not let him see her disappointment or distress. Could she make it that far? Would a body just give out if it became too cold?

Suddenly, Lucinda felt the pressure of William's leg against hers. Where they touched, the chill abated. And though her body continued to shake, she focused on the comfort in that small stretch of calf where their bodies met. It strengthened her resolve to focus on the presence of another human being.

You are not alone. A voice seemed to whisper the reminder. No, she was not alone. Not only was the Lord with her, but she had a husband as well. And she had to endure for him. With that thought, Lucinda straightened her spine, took up the reins, and trained her eyes forward, on her target. Her shivering eased as she focused on pulling her strength from within. From the same place she had the past ten years, that had kept her going through the deepest pain and the cruelest punishments.

With that new focus and resolve, she continued on as her horse took step after step. Until finally, Martin's Station loomed before them. Even in the frigid dark of night, relief bloomed in her chest like the first flower of spring. But the energy was also suddenly sapped from her body. When there was no longer a need for her to be strong, it was a miracle William made it to Lucinda's side to catch her as she slid from her horse.

She thought she heard him utter her name, but could

not be sure. Though her world went dark, she felt William gather her up and lift her as if she weighed no more than a sack of flour. And then there was warmth. Her face stung as the icy air was replaced with a heat that grew with each step that he took. "Over here," she heard a woman's soft voice instruct. Slowly, Lucinda was lowered onto what felt like a coarse hide of hair. Her head rested on a soft surface. A pillow? She must be dreaming.

A groan left her body and she tried to squirm away from the pain that started at her toes. She could not be dreaming, for there was too much pain. "Shh." Someone was beside her, holding her in place. Then a heaviness across her body replaced their touch. Lucinda sighed at the comfort it brought, but a whimper escaped from her as her fingers began the same awful burning as her toes.

"Here. Get some of this in her." A woman's voice. But she did not have the energy to turn and look. Sleep pulled at her, tugging her down into a deep abyss of black oblivion. But the agony pulled her back. Why were they allowing the flames to lick her body? It was a cruel tug of war, wrenched between sweet oblivion and the fiery depths of pain that claimed her inch by inch.

Someone was behind her, lifting her. Lucinda leaned into the comfort of their touch, their strong, solid nearness. Then, a cup was lifted to her mouth, and she was urged to drink. She followed the instruction, but a hot, bitter liquid assaulted her tongue. Her face screwed up, but as the liquid slid down her throat, it brought a settling warmth. So when more was offered, she obliged. Sip after sip she accepted, slowly forgetting the stinging pain that had stretched up her limbs and the weariness that plagued her. Instead, her stomach gurgled as if requesting further sustenance beyond the bitter liquid.

The woman's voice came again, from above her right shoulder. "I believe she is ready for the beans now." There was a smile in her voice.

A rumbled reply vibrated Lucinda's back. The sound warmed and settled her more than the drink. *William.* She would know his deep voice anywhere. And the knowledge that he held her comforted her in a way nothing else could. Her breaths were deep and relaxed as she leaned into his strength and rested.

A conversation began behind Lucinda. "How many?" William's voice.

"Two." Robertson's gruff reply.

"There is room enough. Bring everyone in." The woman's voice interrupted.

"Ma'am, we are over thirty strong, not counting children."

"It will be tight, sir, but it is doable."

Silence ensued, and the door opened a moment later, letting in a cool gust. Then a spoon was brought to her lips. *The beans.* Regaining a bit of her strength at the smell of delicious food, she opened her mouth and ate hungrily what was offered to her. And when her belly was full enough to provide satisfaction, she could fight sleep no longer.

$\sim$

illiam frowned down at his wife. Though she had slipped into a deep, peaceful sleep, he would feel more comfortable if she had finished her bowl of beans first. She needed the nourishment. However, as he peered into the half-empty bowl, his own stomach growled. He glanced from Lucinda, slumped over on his arm in a position that could hardly be deemed comfortable, to the aromatic food sitting next to him. Then, after a moment's hesitation, he proceeded to finish those beans off. And when Mrs. Martin brought him his own steaming portion, he downed it as well.

Only then did he understand why his wife had drifted asleep after her fill of the delicious food. With a belly fuller than it had been in two weeks, a warm fire only feet away, and a heavenly peace and quiet about the cabin, sleep tugged heavily at his eyelids. A peace which was broken moments later when the door opened and other members of the travel party trickled in. William shuddered as the gust of cold air washed over him.

Mrs. Martin was by his side in the next instant. "Is she warm enough to move? We have others that need to be near the fire."

William glanced down at Lucinda, and his insides ached. While he understood the need, he was not ready to move her. It did not seem as if they had been at the fire's side long enough for her frail body to be properly warmed. Still, William carefully slipped her fur-lined glove from her hand and took her slender fingers into his. His breath caught at the feel of her softer hand in his.

Though her fingers were uneven and misshapen, they were a pale, milky white. And beautifully petite. He could easily close her entire hand in his to warm it. Though, to his surprise, her skin was already warm to the touch. He nodded up at Mrs. Martin after pulling his attention away from his wife's hand in his.

"Good. Take her in the back." She nodded toward the rear portion of the building, behind the fireplace at the center of the room. "We will reserve the loft for those that can climb the ladder. And there are plenty of furs back there for bedding. Just never mind the supplies."

With a wave of her hand, the woman was gone again. Though she was young and still newly married, she was the perfect wife for Martin. Their blockhouse had become the last stop on the journey west, where travelers could rest, restock, and have a hearty meal before they passed through the Gap.

William knelt and easily scooped Lucinda into his arms to move her behind the stone chimney which stretched up through the building. Carefully laying her at the edge of the large mound of furs, he gave her one long, last glance before he quickly picked his way back to the front of the cabin. Since not all the families traveled with a stock of furs as he did, he would leave the Martins' supply to those who needed it most. As a long hunter, he had quickly learned the value of keeping several for his own use. So he braved the icy air once more to retrieve his and Lucinda's supplies.

William frowned as he withdrew Lucinda's saddlebag from her horse. On top of the temperature, which had dropped dangerously low, snow now fell in a steady tick.

And the animal, with a coating of white over his fur, shook violently. He feared the equine would not survive the night. *Lucinda will be heartbroken.* He dashed the thought from his mind. Losing animals was a cruel truth of life on the trail.

His own mare seemed to be faring a bit better. Her younger years and stockier build could be her saving grace.

With one last glance, he headed inside with his arms loaded down with saddlebags and rolled furs. Once inside, he stomped off his boots and shook off the chill before he crept back through the crowd to where Lucinda's sleeping form still lay against the back wall. He dropped his load near the rear of the chimney before moving to her side, where he watched for the gentle rise and fall of her chest. Content that she was all right, he used their furs to make one large pallet behind the chimney. As Lucinda's husband, he would do everything in his power to care for her. Even if that meant sharing his bed to ensure she stayed warm through the night.

CHAPTER 11

*L*ucinda's brow furrowed as she slowly became aware of her surroundings, including the heavy log that laid across her torso. *What happened?* Panic rose up her chest and into her throat as she attempted to remember the events of the night before. Visions of a flickering fire danced in her mind, whispers of conversation. Suddenly, her eyes flew open. The block-house. She flipped over in one painful move to see what the weight over her body was and let out a small gasp at the sight. Her hand flew to her mouth, and she cringed at the tiny sound. For William's sleeping form was the culprit behind her discomfort. Her face flushed hot with both embarrassment and joy.

Her husband had chosen to lie next to her. Though, when she looked around, her surprise was dampened. Every inch of the dark cabin seemed filled to the brim with bodies. It was a good chance that William only shared a pallet with her because of the cramped quarters.

He probably did not even mean to put an arm around her. Likely it had been some involuntary reaction in his sleep. But still, here he was, next to her. And she could not help taking a moment to savor his nearness, to allow her eyes to roam over his features freely.

His sandy-brown hair laid unkempt over his forehead. His eyes were closed and his mouth slightly parted as he breathed softly. He was the picture of peace, a sight to behold. A grin spread across Lucinda's face as her gaze followed along the edges of his growing beard, only a slight shade darker than the sandy hair atop his head. She even allowed herself to take in the pockmarks that covered every inch of skin. She resisted the urge to reach up and touch the skin which he had so carefully hidden when they first met. And her heart ached to think of all he had been through.

But after admiring the sight for several moments, it was best to pry herself from her husband's grip. She would not allow either of them the embarrassment of him waking in such an intimate position when William could not possibly have intended it. Plus, the smell of food cooking over the fire had invaded the cabin and drifted to her nose, indicating that she was not the only one awake. So, carefully, she slipped out from under William's thick arm and picked her way around sleeping bodies to the front of the cabin where the dark-haired woman who must be Mrs. Martin had started breakfast.

When Lucinda approached, her hostess glanced up with a smile. "Mornin'. It is not much, but I put some porridge on." She nodded toward the thick substance she stirred in a large pot.

"It smells wonderful." Lucinda smiled. "An' everyone will be grateful for another hot meal."

"I am sure. How are you feeling this mornin'?"

"Warm," Lucinda confirmed. But the response barely scraped the surface of the joy deep inside. For the first time in two long weeks, her frozen body had finally thawed completely to its core.

"Well, if the men insist upon headin' out today, you all deserve a nice, warm meal before you go."

Lucinda glanced toward the door. "Did the weather break in the night?"

"I believe so. But I only cracked the door and peeped out." Mrs. Martin winked in her direction, and Lucinda chuckled. "There is a heap o' snow on the ground, but the sky appears clear. The men should rise and make a decision soon, though."

Lucinda nodded, indecision weighing on her. Was she ready to move on? The cabin was warm and inviting, but quarters were cramped. It would not be long before people grew restless. As if someone had read her mind, a rustle came from her left, and she glanced toward the noise. Her breath caught in her throat.

William stood in the shadows of the flickering firelight, his gaze under his hat trained on her intensely. He did not wear his leather coat but had donned his hat and gloves. Under his scrutiny, heat crept up the back of Lucinda's neck. She was still in her coat, gloves, and shoes. And she could only imagine the state of disarray her hair was in. Why had she not thought to gather herself before she rose? Quickly glancing away, she turned to Mrs. Martin.

"Do you happen to have a washbasin?"

"I do, my dear. Right over there on that table. Though I doubt the water will still be warm." Her lips pulled into an apologetic line.

"That shan't be a problem." Lucinda ducked away and scurried over to the basin, where she slid off her gloves and washed her face with the lukewarm water. Then she worked to gather her hair back into its pins. Once her locks were smoothed into place, she removed her coat and picked her way back to where their furs had been rolled and placed alongside their saddlebags. She carefully laid her outer layer atop the mound, then stood to straighten her clothes. Lucinda frowned at the dingy, rumpled garments. Given the chance, she would change her clothes. But that was quite impossible in a room full of people, even if most still slumbered. And it was much too frigid outside for the task. With one last smoothing of her skirt, she lifted her chin and returned to the front.

~

*W*illiam braced himself as he stepped up into the warm blockhouse. Since the moment he walked out into the snowy morning to find the animal dead, he had dreaded giving Lucinda the news. Once he had shrugged out of his coat, he made his way over to where she handed out bowls of porridge after Mrs. Martin filled them. His eyebrows raised as each person graciously accepted what his wife offered. Had marriage truly been the answer to garnering the trust of the travel party for Lucinda?

"There he is. I told you he would be back soon, dear. No man can resist a hearty meal." Mrs. Martin gave Lucinda a knowing look, and she inclined her head in acknowledgement.

A smile tugged at her lips, adding to her beauty. Her soft-blue eyes drifted to him, and his insides tightened once more. *The horse.* As he stepped up next to her shoulder, he attempted to offer her a smile to hide his motives in conversation. However, the slight wrinkle that appeared on her forehead told him that he had failed miserably. Though, much to his surprise, she played along.

"Has the weather broken, to be sure?" Her question came as she pushed a bowl of porridge in his direction. Perhaps he should decline so his hands would be free to comfort Lucinda when he broke the news? But he did not wish to be rude. So he laid his coat upon the bench and accepted the bowl. As Lucinda handed it to him, she leaned in close and whispered conspiratorially. "She told them they were not goin' to get their porridge if they did not accept it from me." His own smile matched the way the corner of her mouth tugged higher in amusement.

"Good," he confirmed in a low, deep rumble as he gave Mrs. Martin an approving nod. The woman was sure a force to be reckoned with, and he was grateful for her presence in Lucinda's life, if even for a short while. A bit of inspiration and strength might just be what she needed on the trail among the others. "It snowed quite a bit overnight, but the sun is bright and warm today. If it is amenable for you and John, we will stay one more night to restock and regroup, then be on our way."

"Of course. Stay as long as you need. Winter has come

hard and early this year." Mrs. Martin shook her head as finally, she ladled the last bowl of porridge for herself.

William settled onto the bench next to the two women as they started to eat. Silence fell over the trio, but a low murmur could be heard throughout the room.

After several moments, Lucinda leaned close and spoke quietly. "Was there something else ye needed to tell me?"

William cringed inwardly. How was it that this woman could read him so easily? "It can wait until after our meal."

Lucinda visibly paled, and her brow raised. "That serious," she whispered.

William took in a sharp breath of air as he realized his mistake. "No," he responded, but then hesitated. Lucinda peered up at him expectantly, maneuvering herself as she always did to see his face under his hat. Then she reached up and placed a hand on his arm. The warmth and pressure of it on the linsey-woolsey fabric over his arm made the words spill from his mouth. "Your horse did not make it through the night."

Lucinda's pale lips parted. But after a second of processing the shock, "Oh," was all she uttered. Her shoulders sagged as she turned back to her porridge and continued eating.

At first, William was surprised by her lack of reaction. But in truth, it spoke to the woman Lucinda was. She had proven time and again that the she did her best to remain strong and hide her fears. And rarely, it seemed, did the world get the best of her. Still, there was something inside him that wished to ease her pain.

Suddenly, Lucinda glanced back up at him, her eyes wide and damp. "What about yer horse?"

William could not help the smile that tugged at the corner of his mouth. Even in the midst of her own loss, she worried about him. "She made it." He nodded.

A relieved breath escaped his wife's thin body. "Good."

"Yes. You can ride her, or we can ride double."

Lucinda whipped her gaze back to him in an instant. "Oh, I dinnae wish to be any trouble. I can walk."

William contained a grumble at his wife's continued insistence that she was a burden. He gazed down into her beautifully freckled face and resisted the urge to reach up and touch the smooth skin. Instead, he placed a hand on her back. Even through his glove, he could feel her spine. It confirmed for him that staying in place and consuming a few more hearty meals was indeed the correct decision. "It is no trouble," he reminded her, running his hand along her back and leaning close so that she knew he meant what he said.

~

*L*ucinda searched her saddlebag for any additional item that might need mending, but to no avail. She had already inspected each garment thoroughly. That was after she had assisted with dishes and read her Bible for over an hour. With a sigh, her hands dropped into her lap, and she settled back on her heels as she scanned the small mound of belongings before her. Her eye lingered on William's saddlebag. Did he have any clothing that needed mending? Lucinda frowned. Though he may be her husband in name, it would still be inappropriate for her to search William's bags without his permission. And he had disappeared hours ago. With another sigh, she glanced around the room.

Then, with no better idea, she stood and pulled on her coat. Outside, she would either search out her elusive husband or enjoy a walk in the fresh air. While she was grateful for a break from the cold, she could not remain in the stifling cabin any longer. There were too many people, too many eyes, and too little to do to distract herself. The air was stagnant and thick with the smell of unwashed bodies.

Mrs. Martin had been considerate enough to set up a station upstairs behind sheets strung from the ceiling where each person could wash and change. However, that took time and only did so much to ease the smell that had already gathered. Though, at least it had been quite refreshing. Lucinda shrugged her shoulders up and released a contented sigh.

As she stepped out into the afternoon sun, that feeling only intensified. After pushing the door shut behind her, she stopped to take a deep breath of the cool, crisp air. Lucinda's face stretched into a smile as she glanced up at the beautiful blue sky. A slight breeze tickled her cheek with a wisp of hair, but was not frigid enough to work its way under her coat. The mild weather provided a pleasant reprieve from the previously frigid conditions.

Situated at the edge of the Powell River Valley, Martin's Station closely resembled Anderson's blockhouse. Besides the fortified building with a larger top and openings for gun barrels, there was a corral for horses, a blacksmith's forge, and another shed containing wood. That was where her gaze alighted upon her husband.

Leaned back in a straight-back wooden chair, he whittled a small piece of wood. Pale wood chips fell to the snow-covered ground with each deft movement of his blade. Though she could not answer why, Lucinda's heart warmed at the sight. The smile still upon her face, she crossed the distance to the woodshed. She stopped beside him and patiently watched as he added the intricate details to the shape of a horse. Finally, he returned his knife to the sheath at his waist and dusted off the final masterpiece.

"Beautiful," she breathed as he stood and held it out to her.

"It is your horse."

Lucinda gasped and her eyes flew up to William's face. His gaze was still trained on the wooden horse as he spoke again.

"I thought you might like something to remember him by. After all, he carried you to your freedom." William did not look up, but tears of joy filled Lucinda's eyes.

"I suppose he did." Lucinda smiled past her tears, which turned to laughter. "Thank ye." She clutched the carving to her chest as she peered up into William's face. He shrugged a shoulder but still hesitated to meet her gaze. Lucinda stepped forward, closing the gap between them so that he could no longer avoid her eye. "Thank ye for givin' me me freedom. The horse might have carried me all this way, but he would not have done so without ye savin' me first."

William shook his head and moved away from her. His hands clenched into fists as he stared out to where the mountains rose in the distance. The same mountains they would cross through into Kentucky. It was a breathtaking sight, but Lucinda's only concern was her husband.

"Have I done somethin' to offend ye?" Her own brazenness caught her by surprise. She never would have asked such of her father. Instead, she would have cowered out of his way and done all she could to ease his anger. But with William, it was different. He would not become blind with misplaced anger. If something was amiss, she wanted to find the source and correct it.

William blew out his breath, and he shook his head. "No." His voice rumbled as his shoulders sagged. "But how free are you, really? Tethered to me?" When he finally turned his gaze upon her, it was tortured. His brow was furrowed, and pain shone in both his eyes and the set of his jaw.

Lucinda rushed to him. "Of course. Why would ye ever think otherwise?" Her own brows knit together as she stared up into his tan face.

He closed his eyes. "Because you do not know me. Not truly."

She cocked her head to the left and placed a hand on his arm. "Then tell me." Lucinda gestured in the direction of the peaks to their west. "Because I see mountains. Mountains I never would have laid eyes upon or considered crossing without ye." She turned back to her husband and brought her gaze to his face. "An' here, here I see a man who has never degraded me or lifted a hand to harm me. If that is not freedom, then I am not sure what is."

William's hazel eyes sought her then. And she felt as if they truly saw her, all of her. Reflected in them—warmth, admiration, and understanding. Lucinda lost herself in their warm depths as she allowed her husband to work through the turmoil of emotions inside. "My past," he choked out.

"What about it? William, God does not hold our past indiscretions against us. He forgives us."

The pain in William's face as he turned away cut through Lucinda's heart. What was her husband hiding? She longed to know, but she did not press. He needed God's love and forgiveness more than he needed questions at the moment.

Finally, he spoke quietly. "But why would he forgive me when I turned my back on Him years ago?"

"You may have turned your back on Him, but He did not turn His back on you. He has still been walkin' with you every step of the way, waitin' for you to turn around an' see."

William turned back to her and brought a hand to her face. He peered down at her as if willing himself to believe her words. As if grappling for some reassurance that what she spoke was true. He stepped closer and brought his forehead down to meet hers under his hat.

Lucinda breathed in the warmth of his breath. She brought her own hand up against his face and regretted that she had donned her gloves before stepping outside. "William, ye are a good man. No matter what happened before. Ye dinnae have to be that man anymore. Pray tonight. An' rest in God's forgiveness. Then fully embrace the man I know ye to be." She lifted on her toes and placed a gentle kiss on his cheek, right across his pockmarks, above the short beard that prickled her chin. Then she turned and left him without another word.

CHAPTER 12

William shook his head as a gust of cool air whipped against his face and threatened to dislodge his hat. "We should have left yesterday."

"We left when we were supposed to," Lucinda replied confidently from behind him. But, against the front of his chest, the fingers on each of her hands curled. Her pain belied her words. Still, her reassurance provided a meager comfort.

The prior day had been pivotal, after all. William had no desire to change the conversation he had shared with his wife or the time he had spent in solitude, praying. As they set out that morning, it did seem as if a slight weight had been lifted from his shoulders.

But now, clouds gathered and the mild air had turned cool and thick with the threat of precipitation. While he knew the weather of Kentucky and Virginia could be unpredictable, it still astounded him at times how quickly and drastically it changed. Which always proved difficult on the trail.

"Robertson," William called as he urged his mare to pick up her pace. While the palomino lengthened her stride, she seemed hesitant to trot under the extra weight. William clucked his tongue and continued his pressure with his calves. With the extra encouragement, his mare was quick to cover the short distance to Robertson, who waited expectantly.

"We need to consider altering our route so we can overnight at Sand Cave."

Robertson surveyed the sky before nodding his approval. "You know the way better than I do. Want to lead?"

William met the other man's gaze and gave a quick nod.

"I will ride back and advise Donegal." Robertson did not wait for William's reaction before he turned his horse and guided it down the line.

In the last cold snap, the elder gentleman who had been rounding out the back of the travel party had succumbed to the illness that had plagued him over a week. Though Donegal had volunteered to ride at the rear of the travel party in his stead, the man's death had provided a stark reminder of the repercussions of the same conditions that threatened overhead. William curled his arm tighter around Lucinda's frail body.

*L*ucinda closed her eyes and breathed in the aroma of the venison stew she stirred. Her stomach rumbled and her mouth salivated in anticipation of the delicious meal, courtesy of the extra food reserves they had garnered while at Martin's Station.

William echoed her thoughts as he came to sit beside her on the hard-packed sand floor of the cave. "Smells delicious."

Lucinda grinned up at him, though her cheeks heated at his compliment. "Thank ye. It is sure a nice night for a hearty meal," she replied as she nodded toward the large cave opening ahead of them where white snow fell in a steady sheet.

William nodded his agreement but remained quiet. Still, she was grateful for his presence next to her. She could not explain it. Even after having shared a horse all day, she longed to have him at her side. There was a comfortable reassurance in his presence that she could not deny. And she had to admit there had been a greater ease of conversation and interaction between them since leaving Martin's Station. No longer did their marriage seem to settle over them like a burdensome yoke. And for that, Lucinda was all the more grateful. Even if love never grew between them, she could accept a simple comfort in their relationship. After all, someone to spend her life with was a greater blessing than she had ever hoped to receive. She simply did not wish to be a burdensome chore which her husband came to resent.

As she stood to retrieve the tin cups for the stew, she felt less worried about that than she had in a while. On the trail, she had purpose. She filled a cup for Donegal and took it to him, where he sat alone several yards away, staring into the abysmal weather. Robertson must have joined another family, for he was nowhere in sight. Unless Donegal moved next to their fire, she and William might have relative privacy for the night. She filled their cups and settled back in next to him to enjoy the warm meal.

They ate in a comfortable silence for several moments before she spoke. "So we cross into Kentucky tomorrow?"

William nodded, eliciting an excited grin from Lucinda. Her body seemed to hum with the excitement of traveling to a new place she had never seen before. And suddenly she realized she had completely forgotten her pain. Though her body ached with the cold, her thoughts had been so focused on the tasks at hand and looking forward that her pain had become simply a part of the day. An old companion she lived with, but at least for a moment, which did not consume her thoughts. Lucinda breathed a contented sigh. Each day, it seemed more and more that God truly had a plan for her.

As if reading her mind, William spoke up. "Do you want to make Kentucky our home?"

Lucinda's mouth dropped open as she turned to her husband, who stared into the fire, giving nothing away. "Are ye not goin' to remain a long hunter?"

Hunters had often come into her hometown, laden with furs to sell and trade, but they never stayed long in one place. Suddenly, finally, she realized she had seen William before. Not only had he had passed by their home on several occasions, but he had been there that one precious day she had allowed herself to venture outdoors. Only for a moment, she had felt the cool brush of the breeze against her cheeks. But the sight of William had startled her back into hiding. Had God had a plan for them all along? The thought was both comforting and amazing. Could their heavenly Father truly have considered them and planned for them years in advance? How surreal, for such an unworthy person as she? But the Word told her that God knew her before He formed her in her mother's belly. After the years of confinement, she had nearly forgotten she was a precious child of God and that He had a plan for her life. But she did not want those plans to upend her husband's plans or his life.

"I am not sure," William admitted. "But I figure we will want to establish a permanent residence somewhere. Somewhere warm to come home to."

Lucinda's breath caught. *Home. With William.* The idea was incredible. "That does sound nice." She allowed a small smile. William gave a brief nod but remained silent. She ate a few more bites before she ventured another question. "What is Kentucky like?"

"Very much like Virginia. Rolling hills. And caves everywhere."

"Really? Like this?" She glanced around at the large cavern that opened up around them. The sand-colored walls matched the sand floor and held openings along the front of the mountain. Above them, the ceiling boasted reds and greens. It was a masterpiece of God like none other she had ever seen.

William nodded as he followed her gaze. "Though most have rock floors. And there are large rock formations that hang down from the top and rise up from the bottom.

Sometimes they even look like waterfalls made from rock."

In her mind's eye, Lucinda attempted to imagine the surrounding room with the changes William spoke of. "That sounds wonderful." She moved to wash their cups out using the pot of melted snow that sat by the fire. "I would be glad to make a home with you, William, wherever you want."

~

I would be glad to make a home with you...wherever you want. Lucinda's words rolled over and over in his mind, grating deeper into his conscience with each turn. If only his wife knew what kind of man he truly was. She would never be so willing to make a home and life with him. And the guilt gnawed at him with every inch of ground they covered, despite his best efforts to keep his focus on the dangerous crossing over and through the Cumberland Gap. The white rocks of the mountain made travel more difficult, allowing for easier missteps and falls. Clattering could be heard with each foot fall. He should have taken the time to stitch Lucinda a set of moccasins, rather than leaving her to wear her usual low-heeled boots. He gave himself a mental kick as he added another shortcoming to his list of regrets. He should have considered her footwear long before now.

As her foot slipped on a loose rock, Lucinda caught herself on the wet ground with one hand while he held tight to her other. They had long since abandoned riding on the rocky slope, and he held the reins in his right hand

and Lucinda's hand in his left. He would do all he could to keep his wife and their mount safe as they made their way through the Gap.

But the weather was compounding their difficulties. When they had set out that morning, it had seemed as if the weather had cleared. But the higher they climbed, the worse the conditions became. Misting rain covered the already slick rocks in a layer of moisture. And wind gusted against him and Lucinda, threatening to knock them off balance.

William stopped and allowed the gale to gusset his body. He dropped Lucinda's hand but lifted his arm and slid it along her shoulders as she stepped up next to him. With her safely in the crook of his arm, he urged his palomino forward a step and continued on the path with the horse as a buffer against the wind. The three of them walked, huddled side by side, step by slow step. Just before they reached the summit, a cry rent the air. William froze and Lucinda turned her face into him at the blood-curdling sound.

He glanced behind them to locate the source. At the cliff's edge, several people knelt and peered over the edge. One woman consoled another who sobbed and screamed. *Her husband.* William's mouth pulled into a thin line. But with a sad shake of his head, he squeezed Lucinda's shoulders and continued on. Best to move toward safer ground than to linger mourning what was already lost—though he held his wife a bit tighter, his heart heavy.

Even once they had crossed over the rocky peak and started the descent, vigilance was required. William kept

Lucinda on the inside of the trail, farthest from the drop-offs.

They had yet to leave the rocky crags behind when Lucinda slipped. As she collided with William, the impact of her body knocked his feet out from under him. And before he knew it, they were both perched precariously at the edge of a cliff, underneath his mare.

William lifted onto his elbows so that his weight was not crushing Lucinda's thin frame but kept his body between her and the horse, which stepped toward the edge of the precipice, sending a rock clattering down the side of the mountain. "Whoa, mare." He spoke in low tones. The mare's muscles rippled, but she remained in place. "Lucinda, crawl out from under me."

She glanced up at the horse's head, then slowly pulled herself forward on her elbows. She had made it halfway out, her slender waist level with William's eye, when the mare spooked. Letting out a squeal, the mount tossed her head, the whites of her eye showing.

"Go!" William yelled the instruction as the palomino began to back crookedly. One rear hoof stepped off the side of the cliff, and she nearly went down. But thankfully, his horse had enough brains about her to stop and carefully find her footing again.

With Lucinda free, William continued to murmur to the mare. Yet she still pranced in place. Lucinda lowered her hood before she reached for the mare's bridle and started her own sweet talk. Once the horse had visibly calmed, William was able to carefully inch from his precarious position. Suddenly, the palomino panicked again—probably thinking there was a potential predator beneath her. William hissed in pain as a hoof bit into the back of his hand.

But Lucinda kept control of the mare, coaxing her forward to keep the animal from placing its full weight upon his hand and breaking it. Lucinda's gaze shifted from the palomino to his face, even as she continued her sweet murmurings. William nodded, then rolled free and scrambled over to his wife.

"I am so sorry. I tried to keep her still." Lucinda looked up at him with round, apologetic eyes.

But his only concern was her. He looked her up and down for injury before he moved in close and pulled her hood back over her head to fight against the wind that still raged around them. "Are *you* all right?" He took her elbows into his hands, their forearms connecting as he sought the touch that would reassure him she had truly come to no harm.

"Of course," Lucinda replied. Her eyebrows bunched together as her blue-gray eyes peered up into his. He soaked in the sight of her face. Her soft skin showed no evidence of pain, only concern. "What about ye? Yer the one that she stepped on." Lucinda removed her gloves before she reached down and took his hand into hers.

Her touch was so tender that he felt no pain, even as his breath hitched in his chest. Though when she tugged at his glove, it elicited a small, unexpected hiss of pain. Still, William could not remove his eyes from the way her pale fingers moved gingerly as she went about her task. She flipped his hand over to survey each side for injury, then softly ran her fingers over the pock-marked flesh on the back of his tanned hand.

"I dinnae see any bruisin', but I am sure it will come out later." She continued to hold his hand in hers. William only managed a nod in response as he attempted to tame his rapidly beating heart. "Can you make a fist?"

He did as she requested, which he was pleased to find only elicited a minor amount of pain. *Definitely just bruised.* "Thanks to you." The thought slipped out from his mouth.

"Hmm?" Lucinda's wide eyes darted up to his face as if she did not understand his praise.

"You kept her from setting her full weight on it and crushing it."

"Oh." Her mouth formed the word, but the sound barely came out, whisked away in the wind.

William wrapped an arm around Lucinda to protect her from the force of the gale. He held her to him, her small frame tucked into his body and her head under his chin, as the torrent passed.

"We need to get down from here." William reluctantly released his hold long enough to replace their gloves. Then he kept her close to his side as they continued their descent. And as soon as it was safe to ride again, she was pressed against his back and he kept one hand against hers, even as he held his rifle across his lap. The touch of that hand, it was fast becoming as vital to his survival as the gun—a terrifying thought.

CHAPTER 13

*A*group of children danced around in a grove of pines as one of the men played an upbeat fiddle tune. Lucinda chuckled. Even she could not help but tap her toe to the beat of the lively music as a broad grin stretched across her face.

Though Kentucky was still dangerous territory, a sense of celebration pervaded the camp. No matter what woes their futures held, they had made it. Those that remained had made the arduous journey through the Cumberland Gap. And Lucinda was one of them. She stood on Kentucky soil. The thought filled her with a joy and gratitude that bubbled up from her toes and spilled out onto her face.

Tonight, she did not feel the cold. Not only was the chill in the air nothing compared to the brutal winds they had faced on the mountain, but the warm celebration that rippled through camp could thaw any soul. *Maybe even me husband's?* Lucinda raised an eyebrow as that handsome man strode her way. Memories of touching his hand skin to skin spread tingles through her fingers. And she could not help but greet him with a smile.

When he returned it with a genuine grin of his own, a new wave of warmth washed through her chest. "You are here. You are in Kentucky." William held his arms wide, gesturing to the countryside around them, a mix of both barren trees and pines and cedars, which filled the breeze with a heavenly scent befitting the festive mood of the night.

"I think I like it." Lucinda pretended to look around thoughtfully before she turned her smile upon William.

"Good."

Though he crossed his arms over his broad chest as he settled in next to her to watch the festivities, his closeness warmed her. With barely a space between their shoulders, a pleasant tingle stirred through her body and flushed her cheeks. Did she imagine it, or were they growing closer daily?

~

*W*illiam glanced Lucinda's way as she knelt next to the fire to dry. The corner of his mouth tipped up against his will. She had been much more relaxed when she had been on the river crossing that morning. His wife seemed to be settling into the frontier life, and he had to admit, it looked good on her.

As if sensing his gaze, she glanced up and offered him

a smile before she turned to the task of sorting through their belongings. Though most of the supplies had been taken across the river on a makeshift raft, it was still imperative to check their stores for any dampness.

Seeing Lucinda growing into her new life stirred a strange mix of emotions deep in his gut. While her joy brought William happiness, guilt still gnawed at the edge of his conscience. As long as Lucinda did not know the full truth about him, they lived a lie. Every day, every hour, he allowed their affection for one another grow. And yet, if Lucinda knew the truth, would it harden her heart to him forever? It would be deserved. He turned with that bitter thought to gather additional firewood.

Still, William found it difficult to shatter the illusion that grew between them. The thought of a future with Lucinda in it continued to unfold, giving him hope and a reason to live. How could he risk losing the admiration and respect he saw in her face? Though, deep down, he knew that was selfish. She deserved to know, and he was deceiving her by keeping the truth from her. A low growl of frustration rumbled out of his chest before he reminded himself that he needed to pay quiet attention to his surroundings.

With a quick scan of the land, he headed back toward camp, his arms laden down with logs. His gut clenched as Lucinda greeted him with yet another beautiful smile.

"Thank ye." She nodded to his load. "Venison will be ready soon."

William returned her nod as the delicious smell drifted to his nose. The venison was a delightful change in pace from the prior two weeks—one he was grateful for. But he could barely meet his wife's gaze.

"I will water the horse in the meantime," he made excuse as he turned away.

Why had the weight of this secret settled so heavily over his chest since they had entered Kentucky? Was it because every step took them closer to their future? Closer to building a home? Either way, he could not contain it much longer.

~

*T*he next day, Lucinda leaned against the maple behind her, her hips wedged into the natural seat created by its large roots and her gaze trained on the Bible in her lap. Cold wind nipped at her cheeks as she attempted to focus on the words before her. But she had been at the task long enough to grow restless. And her husband sitting several yards away, propped against his own tree, was a thorough distraction. Her attention shifted to his strong form, though she kept her head bent as if she were still reading.

Beneath a bright blue sky, William leaned against a wide oak, whittling on a stick he had recovered nearby. Sunday rests were a pleasant break from the demands of the trail, but one could easily find themselves bored, with little to do.

Lucinda's joints had grown stiff from sitting, and a walk would ease them. Though it was a long way off, she wished for spring, with budding trees and blooming flowers. It would make for a much more pleasant stroll.

Would her husband entertain her idea of a walk, though? Her lips pressed together as she watched him. Though he had seemed quite congenial when they first arrived in Kentucky, he had since withdrawn from her. In fact, he had barely uttered a word to her in the past two days. Sure, William sat where he could watch out for her. But that was out of obligation. Had he only been so pleasant because of their near-miss crossing through the gap? Had he remembered that he never intended to marry her? Or was there something else at play?

Lucinda sighed before she carefully raised from her position. Clutching her Bible to her chest, she approached William.

At first, it seemed he would ignore her as he continued to take bits off the length of wood with his knife. Rhythmically. Methodically. But after a moment of silence, he peered up at her from beneath his hat.

"Would ye take a walk with me?"

William visibly swallowed. Lucinda's heart plummeted. What had happened between them?

"Sure." William seemed to have recovered as he dropped his whittling to the ground and stood. He even slipped an arm behind her back as they started out.

Lucinda knew not where she was headed, but she walked down the rise, away from camp. Leaves crunched underfoot as they wove between barren trees toward a stand of pines. She focused on keeping her steps even and regular. She continued to adjust to the fur-lined moccasins William had given her their first night in Kentucky. Even with his silence, it brought joy to her heart to wear them.

"Thank ye again for the moccasins." Lucinda did not glance at her husband as she spoke but simply kept her feet aimed toward the green pines.

"You are welcome. Again, I only wish I had made them for you sooner."

Lucinda ventured a glance in William's direction. Though he looked ahead, she offered him the smallest of smiles. "Well, I still appreciate the gesture. They feel much nicer than those stiff, uncomfortable boots." While her feet had often seemed as if they were wedged into a vice in her too-small boots, they felt as if they could breathe in the moccasins. It was almost as if she were barefoot. And yet, her feet stayed warm as root and twig rolled beneath them.

"I am glad for that."

Lucinda's mouth pulled tight at William's abrupt response. She skirted the edge of the pines, not sure of her next word or step, only knowing she wanted to continue walking with William. Anything to return to their old, comfortable ways, to ease the tension chorded between them.

Memories of the day a couple weeks earlier when she and William had taken a similar walk at Anderson's block-house came back to her—the day she had agreed to come west with William. It seemed a lifetime ago now. On that day, she never would have dreamed of all that would result from that single choice. But now it all seemed to hang in the balance as a deafening, heartbreaking silence surrounded them.

Suddenly, William stopped her with a hand on her

arm. She looked up expectantly, but his gaze darted to their surroundings. "We should not venture too far from camp."

Lucinda glanced at the seemingly open land around them. "Oh." Her gaze settled on his face. But still, he looked back toward camp instead of at her. Tears pricked the backs of her eyes, but she blinked them back. "Aye. Ye are right," she replied tightly as she turned back. Her arms hugged tighter around her body.

While she had questioned his distant nature before, it seemed futile to continue to do so. After all, William had never wanted to marry her. Though it had seemed something had shifted between them, that some bond or affection had grown, she should never have come to expect anything besides resentment. She was a burden that had been forced upon him, and he must have realized such. Still, it did not ease the ache in her chest.

Lucinda trudged back toward camp. And though, with nothing else to focus on, she slowly became aware of the pain in her joints again, she continued on, step after miserable step.

When they reached the place where William had sat whittling, he stopped but Lucinda continued on. "Lucinda," he called after her. When she turned, there was a wrinkle in the skin between his brows, and his mouth was drawn.

"I need to prepare supper." She answered the unasked question reflected in his face. He hesitated, and she thought he might say more. Her heart longed for it. But instead, he simply nodded.

~

*W*illiam ran a hand over his mare's thick winter coat, his gloved fingers dark against the creamy gold, before he turned back toward camp. Lucinda knelt beside the fire, her hands held out to soak in the warmth of the flames. She seemed so serene as she wiggled her fingers before the dancing orange light. A pang of guilt sliced through him because he knew he had to ruin the moment and steal her happiness. His mouth pulled into a deep frown as he forced his feet forward. At the crunch of leaves underfoot, Lucinda quickly dropped her hands and picked up the pan of venison beside her.

But before she could move the food over the fire, William covered her hand with his and stayed it. When she turned to him expectantly, the sight of her pale skin in the flickering firelight took his breath away. Its creamy softness beckoned him. Her hair, falling loose from its tight knot, blazed a reddish gold. "I want to show you something," he managed to say.

Wordlessly, Lucinda stood and allowed him to lead her away from the campsite, into the dusky woods. William moved slowly, deliberate in his choice of path as she followed behind. With a mostly cloud-covered sky, dark gathered quickly. His breath came in spurts of white cloud before him, and his heart beat rapidly in dread of the conversation that was to come. But beyond the barren tree branches dusted with snow, the gurgling of water drifted to his ears on the chilly breeze. And he followed its call.

Finally, thick layers of dead grass and leaves gave way to a sandy shore. William found a downed tree, brushing the snow from the rough bark before he settled onto it, then held a hand out to his wife. When she slipped her gloved hand into his, he drew her down next to him, wrapping an arm around her while he still could.

He closed his eyes for only a second as he savored the feel of her slender body pressed against his. But then he forced his attention to the expansive river before them. Pale light from the partially obscured moon reflected off its glassy surface, creating the illusion that the deep black waters did not move as swiftly as they truly did.

Next to him, Lucinda stiffened. "We cross that tomorrow?" Her voice was tentative as she whispered the question aloud.

William frowned before he drew her closer to him. "Yes," he confirmed in a quiet rumble. He turned his gaze from the massive river that caused her trepidation and settled it on her face, as if he could comfort and reassure her with a single glance. But as those timid blue eyes met his, it was he who was lost in the comfort of her face. While darkness swam all around them, her milky-white skin and luminous eyes seemed to draw the moonlight. Her pale-pink lips were slightly parted as her warm breath slipped out into the cold night air and intermingled with his.

Lucinda's face was mere inches from his, and her body melded perfectly into his as she leaned into his strength. He longed to close the gap and press a sweet kiss to those precious lips. But instead, he ripped his gaze free and pulled her fully to him, his chin resting gently against the top of her head. William drew a deep breath into his body. He could not abandon his senses. For the moment of truth had come.

But before he could shatter the illusion of love that enveloped them, Lucinda spoke. "When we are crossing, I fear the water's strength. Its untamed need to rush forward and consume all in its path. But in your arms...in your arms, I feel safe."

The words penetrated his soul and pierced his wounded heart. He swallowed and shook his head. Though he wanted nothing more than to spend his days doing all he could to keep Lucinda safe, he could not allow her to continue with her delusions. As much as it tore him apart, he forced the words past his lips. "You are not as safe with me as you believe."

Lucinda pulled back and stared at him in bewilderment. Her blond brows lowered as his hands fell away from her. When she spoke, her words were laced with apprehension. "Why not?".

The words stuck in his throat. "I told you. I am not a good man." William's voice was raw with emotion as he turned his gaze out over the dark waters. He could not bear to watch as he broke his own wife's heart.

"An' what have ye done that is so terrible?" Her slender hand came up to rest on his arm, causing him to tense.

"I killed my sister." William spat the words as he dropped his head into his hands. Cold air invaded the space between them as truth collided with reality and Lucinda drew back.

"Wh-what do you mean?"

"It was supposed to be me. She was so young, with so much life to live. I was grown. When I woke up, she was already gone. It was too late." The confession tumbled out of him like water bursting from a dam. He shook his head and pressed his eyes shut against the dampness there.

Lucinda was quiet for several moments. Then, to his surprise, she did not desert him or lash out in anger or disgust. No, his heavenly little wife slid closer to him, her warmth edging into the dark corners of his soul. Suddenly, her bare fingers met with the side of his face in the sweetest touch. Their soft length slid over the repulsive, pock-marked flesh of his cheek that had forced him to live beneath the shadow of a hat. But there was no hesitation, no quiver to her touch. Instead, it was almost reverent. "Smallpox," she finally breathed.

William nodded. The dreaded disease that had taken everything from him. His sister, then his family and way of life. And left him a ghost of the man he could have been.

"Oh, William. That was not yer fault."

William's brows pulled together as he turned and looked his wife square in the face. "But it was. I read to her every single night. Even when I began to feel ill, she begged me to read to her and I relented." He shook his head. "I should not have given in. The next day, I could not leave the bed. I became so ill, I was not aware of anything. Even when she took sick herself. And I was not there, could not do a thing to help her. When I awoke... she was gone." He pleaded with Lucinda to understand, to realize how despicable he truly was. He could only live with himself once he knew she had seen, and fully comprehended, the deepest, darkest depths of who he was.

But once again, Lucinda surprised him as she took his face in her hands. Her soft skin wrapped him in warmth and tenderness as she gazed into his eyes. "It was a miracle you survived. There is nothing you could have done to save her." She shook her head. "I know it makes no sense that God called her home so young. But William..." Lucinda's voice broke, and the sound touched a tender place within his heart, coaxing it to life. "I do not wish to know where I would be today if God had taken you instead."

William was left dumbfounded. As he stared into the blue-gray eyes that held his, he could see the sincerity of her words. Despite the reprehensible truths he had spewed, love and acceptance filled her gaze. Raw gratitude overflowed from her being and slid through her fingers into her warm touch.

William searched her face for something he understood. Some sort of disdain or disappointment. But he found none. Not even the tiniest speck of hesitation laced her features. *How?*

"You do not despise me?"

Lucinda's face tilted as one side of her mouth tipped up in a smile. Her hands dropped from his face, allowing the cold air to replace them. The breeze lifted him with a refreshing newness as she instead brought a hand up to his arm. "Why would I despise ye for something ye could not control?"

William opened his mouth to speak, but no words came out. His shoulders sagged as realization washed over him. He had blamed himself for his sister's death for years, carrying the weight as a shackle around his neck. Yet now, as he searched for a reason, some way he could have prevented it, he could not think of anything. As he watched Lucinda, he felt ten times lighter.

"But I lied and kept this from you." He had expected her anger and resentment for so long, he was not sure what to do without them.

Compassion welled within his wife's face. "William, have ye told anyone else in all these years?"

William blinked. "No."

Lucinda drew nearer to him, resting her other hand on his leg. "Ye entrusted me with a burden ye have carried alone all these years. With yer innermost secret. How could I ever be ill with ye when ye have allowed me closer than any before?" Her hand squeezed reassuringly as her gaze searched his.

William could not speak. God had used the very thing that he thought would drive them apart, that he had believed made him unworthy, to create a deeper, more beautiful connection with his wife. As the most beautiful woman in the world peered up at him with eyes the color of a clear blue sky tinted by the gray of a coming storm, thoughts of a real future with her began to materialize within the depths of his mind. Without a further thought, he lifted her into his lap and brought his mouth down to hers in a kiss filled with both gratitude and wonder.

Though their lips were cold at first contact, the kiss

bloomed and grew as their bodies responded to one another. Lucinda's lips were as soft and perfect as he had always imagined, pliant against his as she leaned into his touch. And though a bleak, frigid darkness cloaked the world around them, William felt only the warmth and promise of a spring day.

CHAPTER 14

$\mathcal{A}$s Lucinda stood staring out at the blue-green waters of the wide Cumberland River, her stomach swirled, much like the shallows at the river's edge. A million emotions and considerations tumbled inside her, creating a nauseating roil that did little to distract her from the coming crossing. Her lips pressed together as she turned her attention from the icy depths to the men working down the river from where she stood.

Though the sun was warm, winter had settled heavily in the air, and the guides had agreed a raft crossing would offer everyone's best chance of survival. William labored alongside Donegal, Robertson, and several other men as they worked to form a makeshift raft as quickly and efficiently as possible. William stood and shook his head before wiping the back of his arm across his forehead. Her mouth flattened further. With the raft meant to carry more than simply supplies, the vessel must be both sturdy and reliable, as well as easily maneuvered by ropes. The crossing would be difficult and require a substantial amount of time. Neither of which excited Lucinda.

William had reminded her how to shoot his rifle that morning before he set to work with the other men. Even now, she held it at her side. William feared, because the crossing would take much of the day, the travel party would be left vulnerable to attack.

Lucinda took a deep breath before she turned and surveyed her surroundings, as she had seen William do so many times before. On either side of the river, the land rose, forming what would be a picturesque valley at any other time of the year. In fact, it was still impressive with the dark, barren trees spotting the snow-dusted ground. Would their vantage point help prevent attack? Though the enemy would have the high ground, it would be difficult to surprise their party. Especially seeing as several men had been reserved from the raft building to stand guard. Lucinda prayed so.

She sighed, and her gaze slid back to her husband's form where he was bent over a tree branch, sawing the branches from its length. He appeared strong and powerful as he worked, and she could not help but admire him with a small grin. The warmth of the sun seeped deeper into her body and warmed her cheeks from the inside out as she remembered the kiss they had shared the night before. Her lips tingled as she recalled the sensation of his mouth pressed against hers as emotions overflowed between the two of them.

As perfect as the moment had been, it brought her heart even greater joy to consider that she and William might now be on the path to a true, loving marriage. Since the day they had met, William had held the conviction that he was not good enough for her. But with his secrets laid bare and her acceptance unwavering, would he relinquish such a foolish thought? Or would he still feel as though she could not, or should not, love him?

Another sigh escaped as Lucinda pulled her attention away from William. She could ponder all day and it would yield her no answers. Finding the root of a massive oak to settle onto, she closed her eyes. *Lord, it is all in Your capable hands. I will trust the fate of my marriage to Thee.* As she breathed deeply, she did her best to mentally hand her concerns over to the one who held all. It was a task that always seemed easier said than done. Nevertheless, her chest felt lighter as she reopened her eyes to the bright morning sun.

Her heart plummeted as her gaze landed once again on the mighty river that cut through the valley. *Trouble for today.* Her lips pulled into a frown, and her hands tightened around the barrel of the rifle laid across her lap. The gun weighed heavily on her thighs as the worries it represented tugged at her heart.

~

William's arms tensed against the pressure of the rope as he held onto it for dear life. He dug his heels into the soft, sandy dirt at the edge of the river as he and the others behind him hauled backward as hard as they could.

"Heave!" Robertson bellowed from up the river, where another line of three men fought to keep the large raft from careening off course. William's heart pounded in his chest, and sweat intermixed with river water from his own crossing in front of the raft. But his eyes never wavered from Lucinda's pale face as her fingers dug into the bark of the logs on either side of her.

Though he had insisted she come across with the first wave, the fear etched into her face and the groan of the ropes made him regret the decision. The first wave had the fewest men on this side of the river working to pull the raft across, fighting the current every inch of the way. William swallowed as he placed one hand over the other, careful not to lose his grip.

Slowly, the raft inched closer. Even so, Lucinda seemed a world away. Not only was the Cumberland River powerful, but it was expansive. And it dwarfed both the raft and their efforts. He and the men who had brought across the front set of ropes had to enter its depths farther upriver than where they intended to land. William had felt the full force of the current as his palomino had poured her heart and strength into swimming him across the distance. If it was within his power, he would not allow that same swift water to carry his wife away.

So he continued to place hand over hand in slow, diligent progress as he worked one boot-covered foot back a step, onto more solid ground. There, he dug in his heel and followed with the other foot. The men behind him did likewise. That was, until the man in the back slipped on a patch of snow.

William heard the "umph" as the man fell, then felt legs collide with his as Donegal was taken down as well. William's eyes widened, and for a moment, all he saw was the water rushing toward him as his feet gave way. But he scrambled with all he was worth to find a foothold. And finally, at the very edge of the water, his heel lodged behind a rock. His and the other men's forward motion halted as they dug in with heels and elbows wherever they could.

A minuscule wave of relief washed over him. His gaze flew up to confirm Lucinda was still safe on the raft and locked on her as she crouched on all fours, her eyes wide. A weight seemed to release from her shoulders, and she settled back on her heels. In the panic of the moment, she had forgotten her own fears in favor of his safety. In fact, it appeared she would have crawled right off the edge of the raft had she believed she could save him. Something warmed and twisted within his heart. How could this incredible woman care so deeply and unwaveringly for him?

"Come on, men." Donegal's gruff voice came from behind him as the man struggled to stand.

William followed suit. He kept a tight hold on the rope as he fought to stand while still maintaining control of the raft, which now floated at a crooked angle to the shore. His knees found the rock-strewn bank. With a grunt, he slowly worked his way upright, planting one foot first, then the other. Then he and the two men behind him eased up the bank.

Finally, the raft inched its way closer once more. The span of water between the sandy, rocky shore and the sawed ends of the logs grew smaller and smaller. When the raft finally ran aground, he and the men worked quickly to secure the ropes to nearby trees. William could hardly concentrate on the task, for people had begun to disembark. He glanced back to ensure Lucinda had not been knocked into the river by an overzealous raft mate. As soon as the knot was secure, he turned and sought his wife's face. After she tumbled off the corner of the raft, she stumbled across the soft bank and into his arms.

Her eyes were wide as she gripped his forearms tightly. Her breath came in quick spurts, and her eyes locked onto his. "Are ye all right?"

William circled his arms around her as he pulled her into his embrace. He hugged her slight body against his to confirm to himself that she was indeed safe. His brows knit together as he looked down into her beautiful face, etched with worry. "Of course I am. Are you?"

Lucinda's head cocked to the side as her own brow wrinkled. "Aye," she replied, as if he should already know.

"Good." Words seemed to fail William. He brushed back the hood of her fur-lined cloak. Wisps of reddish-gold hair sprang free and were caught by the wind, taking his breath away. His wife was as stunning as a spring day with all the world in bloom. And she infused within him the same warmth and hope.

Could God have truly blessed him with the love of this remarkable woman? His insides twisted and his mouth dipped into a frown. Though he might not be responsible for his sister's death, he was still guilty of turning his back on God. Why, then, would the Almighty show him such abundant grace as to bless him with such a bride as Lucinda?

"Time to send her back!" Robertson called across the

valley, pulling William from his thoughts long enough to urge Lucinda into the trees behind him.

"Find our packs and start a fire," he urged. "Far enough from the riverbank in case of flood." Though the skies were clear, one should always be prepared. As he released her from his arms, worry gnawed at him. His gaze followed her as she walked away. He could never be prepared for all that could happen on the trail. So how, then, could he ever keep his wife safe?

~

*L*ucinda's lips twisted as she trudged across the thick flooring of dead leaves dusted with snow. It crunched beneath her with each irritated step she took, reflecting her mood. Though William had seemed as eager to greet her as she had him, had she misread the moment?

For mere seconds after learning that she had safely made the river crossing, he had withdrawn from her with a frown. Hurt twisted deep inside her chest, an old familiar rejection that stung more than she cared to admit. Perhaps she should not raise her hopes regarding her marriage. If she expected nothing, she could save herself disappointment. A sigh escaped, and her arms flapped at her sides before she bent to gather firewood from beneath the branches of an old pine.

As she straightened, a gunshot rang through the air, nearly causing her to drop her load. She whipped toward the sound, her heart pounding in her ears. *William.*

Without thought to her safety, Lucinda dumped the

wood and ran back through the trees as fast as her unevenly matched legs would allow. As she neared the river's edge, she slowed and ducked behind a wide oak. Without knowing the cause of the gunshot, she needed to be careful not to stampede into a dangerous situation. That would do no good. However, a familiar voice drifted to her ears. Lucinda then peered around the trunk. Unfortunately, more trees hid most of the scene from her view. A boy who appeared a couple years younger than herself stood staring at the ground as the voice yelled. Robertson? Her brow lowered, and she darted from behind a tree, only to collide with a hard surface. She staggered backward but gasped when two large hands gripped her arms. Before she could focus on the substantial form before her, her subconscious mind darted back to the times her father had gripped her similarly. She was just about to cower from the expected blow when a familiar voice cut through her fear.

"There you are," William breathed. His right hand slid down to take hers, while his left came up to nestle her forehead against his under the worn brim of his hat.

Though the moment was heart-warming, she did not allow herself to linger in the feeling. Instead, she pulled back. "What happened?"

William's hand slid from the back of her neck as he let out a groan. "One of the young men on guard duty was not alert to his surroundings, spooked at an unexpected noise, and managed to shoot Robertson." William shook his head.

Lucinda's eyes widened and her stomach dropped. "Is he...?"

"No, no." William shook his head. "It was only a through and through in the flesh of his shoulder." William's fingers moved over the back of her hand, detectable through her glove. A warm tingle worked its way up her spine. "I did not know where the bullet went from there, though." His golden gaze bore into hers with a heat that took her breath away.

Indeed, she had been foolish to question whether William cared for her. While he might not love her in the way she longed for, he cared deeply. And for that, she could be grateful.

CHAPTER 15

*A*pprehension prickled up the back of William's neck as he led his mare the short distance to the creek after making camp the next day. He stopped and carefully surveyed his surroundings. But finding nothing amiss, he cautiously continued on toward the stream where he would have to break through the ice to water the palomino.

His mouth pressed into a thin line. Fall was long forgotten, replaced with a heavy winter that threatened to stall travel. Thick clouds gathered overhead, and a bitter wind wound its icy tendrils around the exposed flesh of his upper neck. More snow was to come, and they had yet to make it to the caves near the Rockcastle River.

Still, the nagging unrest deep in his core went beyond concern over the weather. Though he could not put his finger on what, something had felt off all day. As he reached the stream that cut through the hillside, William took another look around before he pulled out his hatchet and hacked away a top layer of ice.

After he returned the tool to its place on the saddle, he gave the horse her head and leaned his arms across her back. Could his agitation be due to the tumult of emotions that had passed between him and Lucinda the past couple of days? His gut twisted tighter, as if to answer his own question.

How was it, that with all laid bare between him and his wife, the future seemed more uncertain than ever? He sighed and leaned his head back, turning his gaze heavenward. The gray clouds rolled and gathered, much like the storm brewing within him. He had come clean, showing Lucinda the deepest, darkest corners of his soul, and she had not flinched. If anything, she had drawn closer. And he still could not wrap his head around it.

Lucinda's words had been encouraging. But could he truly believe them? It seemed too much to ask that anyone, even the Lord, could forgive him of his misdeeds. He groaned and placed his head in his hands.

But one sentence kept coming back to him over and over. *I do not wish to know where I would be today if God had taken you instead.* When William considered the situation from her perspective, he was grateful for that fateful night. For he did not wish to imagine either where Lucinda would be if he had not rescued her from her father's plans. He could delude himself into thinking that someone else would have saved her, or that whichever drunkard had won her hand would have been kind to her. Deep inside, he knew those things would not have happened. No. God had placed William in her father's path that night, and God had brought him to Lucinda.

Could it be, Lord? Hope took root in his soul as he consulted the Heavenly Father he had neglected for so long. *Did You use me for good? Even after I ran from You for so long?* Mixing with the hope, shame crept in again. God had loved him, provided for him, and protected him over the past five years. And yet, he had run from it and denied it. Why had God used someone as unworthy as he? Another sigh slipped past his lips. Was that not what the Lord had done for all of time?

William scrubbed his hands over his face. But could he embrace the truth? Could he let go of the past and accept the future before him? He had to try. If for no other reason than for Lucinda's sake. She was a faithful servant of the Lord, a beautiful, innocent soul that deserved a wonderful future.

William straightened and took up the reins to lead his mare back to camp. That night, he would ask his wife what she truly wanted from their marriage. The thought of a genuine marriage still did not sit well with him, but he trudged on, anyway, as large white flakes of snow started to fall from the sky. Beside him, his palomino stopped, her nostrils flaring. His brow lowered, but he had no time to consider the cause of her distress.

A piercing cry rent the air, and William dropped the reins as he set out at a run. *Lucinda.* He slid to a stop at the edge of camp. Two braves adorned with feathers and bone butchered anyone that dared to breathe. Blood and bodies littered the ground. His heart pounded in his ears as he crouched behind a tree. His eyes scanned, but Lucinda was nowhere in sight.

No. He had left his rifle with Lucinda and his hatchet strapped to the saddle. How could he save his wife when he had no weapon? He glanced around but found nothing to aid his efforts. He stifled a growl as he leaned his back against the tree and closed his eyes.

When he reopened them and peered back around the tree trunk, a tall, slender brave with his face painted black and red knelt over a woman, a wild gleam in his eye. William had to do something. Running forward, he tackled the brave to the ground. He scrambled up to where he could land a punch, but a tanned arm came up to block him, tomahawk in hand. William caught the wrist and used the forward momentum to press the brave's hand into the ground, where his grasp on the tomahawk loosened. William grabbed it and raised it above his head for a strike.

But before he could inflict a blow, something collided with his shoulder and toppled his weight forward. The man beneath him bucked and brought his feet up, sending William sailing above his head. He met the hard earth with a thud. He blinked and attempted to sit up, but the burning pain in his shoulder spread, and his vision became foggy. The blunt end of a tomahawk flew toward him, but the hand he tried to raise never moved. Instead, he stared in confusion before his world went black.

∼

*L*ucinda covered her mouth to stifle a scream as she watched the scene unfold from behind a stand of pines up an embankment. Her body shook with the need to move, to do something. But that would only result in her capture or death. As the men marked with war paint strung William's legs together and strung them from a bare tree branch to drag him along behind them, her chest burned with the desire to go after him. But there were six braves, and she was only one woman. A crippled woman, at that. Tears rolled down her face, but she fought back the sobs that threatened to tear from her.

Instead, she waited silently for the attackers to leave with their three prisoners as icy snowflakes fell against her face. And only once they had been gone for some time did she turn her back to the tree trunk and give in to the sobs that racked her body. Hopelessness and regret washed over her in wave after wave as the images of William falling and being taken away replayed in her mind. Though she had wanted to warn him when she noticed his approach, she had not known how to draw his attention without revealing their positions. And when she had decided to leave the safety of the tall pine, she had only taken a half step in his direction when he had tackled Elizabeth's attacker.

More sobs came as she considered the scene that lay behind her. She would have to face it. Have to face the bodies and the blood. But for the time being, she wallowed in the torment of desperate emotions. And she wept for all that was lost.

And in the deep, dark depths of her despair, she began to wonder why she had run for cover when the attack began. After all, what good did it do for her to have been spared? She had been unable to stop the bloodshed. Unable to stop William's capture. And now she sat behind a grove of pines with no hope and no plan. Could she even survive on her own? The empty, white forest before her swam in her tear-filled vision. And all that met her ears was an eerie silence. Desperation and fear cut deep into her being and spurred another round of muffled sobs as she dropped her head into her hands.

She cried until there were no tears left to cry. Until her insides were as numb as her fingers and toes were from the cold. Lucinda leaned her head back against the tree, her eyes closed and arms propped on her knees, her hands hanging in the frigid air that seeped through her gloves and claimed her fingers. *Lord, why was I spared?*

When something nudged the left side of her hand, she nearly jumped out of her skin. Her eyes flew open as her back grated against the tree trunk. But the sight that met her did not scare her. Instead, it brought a ripple of joy that sliced through her despair. Standing, she cautiously offered her hand to William's beautiful golden mare. A smile spread across her face as the animal whuffled her hands with her warm breath and then stepped closer. Lucinda closed the gap, wrapping her arms around the horse's neck and burying her face in the thick, cream-colored fur. Cold, happy tears slipped down her cheeks.

And as she hugged the sturdy animal that nuzzled her back, the tightness in her chest eased a bit. She could not regret her decision. She could not. For she had done the one thing William would have wanted her to do—escape. Lucinda stroked the mare's soft fur and leaned into her strength, drawing deep, calming breaths into her lungs.

Even if William did not love her, he cared for her. And she could not bear the thought of him seeing her lying down there like the other women, their scalps shorn from their heads. A cry bubbled up in her chest, and she clasped her hands over her mouth to stop both it and the acid that rose from her stomach. She squeezed her eyes shut as two tears streaked down her cheeks.

The mare brought her nose up to Lucinda's neck, where her warm breath puffed out of her nostrils onto Lucinda's skin. A smile tugged at the corners of Lucinda's mouth before duty sobered her. No matter how it churned her stomach, she had to face the camp. She shivered against the frigid wind that rustled the pine branches and kicked up a cloud of snow. Then she picked up the palomino's reins and took a deep breath.

When she stepped forward, so did the mare, staying right at her side—almost like a physical reminder of God's presence. But when they reached the first body at the edge of camp, she steeled herself for the horse to balk. The acrid smell of blood filled the air, crinkling her nose and causing her stomach to roil. She brought the back of her hand to her nose as her eyes filled with tears.

Lucinda looped the palomino's reins over a branch and focused on the snow-dusted ground as she moved forward. With shaking hands, she checked each body for life before she closed wide, staring eyes. And because she did not possess the strength to dig even a single grave in the frozen ground, she covered each body with a blanket or fur. Silent tears poured down her face as she reunited children with their mothers.

As she moved through camp, Lucinda doused the dying embers of each campfire with handfuls of fluffy white snow. Just before the attack, Donegal had instructed them to quiet and put out their fires. Her heart sank and her brows lowered as she considered the man who had tried to warn their group. She did not remember seeing him taken away as a prisoner or covering his body. What had become of him? Had he escaped, or was his fate that of the many others she had tended? She sent up a silent prayer before she continued on.

As inappropriate and invasive as it felt, once the last blanket was laid, Lucinda had to turn to searching through supplies. Guilt gnawed at her as she reached into packs and saddlebags, but food and ammunitions would be imperative to her journey. And she made sure to leave all personal effects as they were. That was, except for hers and William's. Once she had completed her rounds, she moved to where their campfire was now covered in a powdery layer of snow and knelt beside their saddlebags. She packed all she could and retied and loaded everything as she had seen William do so many times. Then she tossed another saddlebag containing the extra supplies over the palomino's neck. The mare let out a small grunt but stood still as Lucinda carefully mounted, her own body loaded down with weapons.

Astride the horse, she hesitated. Where to go from here? She could only imagine that William would want her to leave him behind and do all she could to ensure her own survival. Most likely, he would pack her up and send her back to Martin's Station.

But she could not do that. Lucinda shook her head, and without hesitation, turned the horse in the direction the prisoners had been taken. She had to attempt to save William, even if it meant her own death. *I cannot leave behind the man I love.*

With tears in her eyes, she took a shuddering breath. Had she come to love William without even meaning to? The thought stole the air from her lungs. But the wrenching pain in her chest when she considered life without him told her it was the truth. So, despite all seemingly lost, she raised her chin as she sat tall astride the mare and gave the horse her head. "We have to save him," she whispered into the wind.

Lord, please guide our steps. And please make the impossible possible.

CHAPTER 16

*A*s darkness began to shroud them, Lucinda's shoulders sagged lower than her spirits. Her eyes scanned for a place to make camp, but she had been unable to find somewhere protected from the snow that continued to fall off and on. Finally, she spotted a pine at the base of a rock wall. She slipped from the mare's back and winced at the pain that seared through her feet as she landed, gripping the saddle to steady herself. Then, she moved carefully and stiffly as she retrieved the canteen and allowed both herself and the horse a drink. Slipping her gloves from her fingers, she ignored the pain of the freezing water against her fingers as she did her best to cup some of it for the animal.

A heavy sigh escaped her lips, and tears formed in her eyes. Why did every load seem more difficult to bear without William at her side? She blinked back her tears and moved to finding firewood. The thought of making a campfire and alerting those that took William to her presence sat uneasily with her. But there was no way she would survive the night otherwise.

So she followed the same steps she had every night, quickly and ably starting the fire. Thank goodness, William had taught her a few things through their time together. That may well have been because he knew the perils of Kentucky. In a way, it warmed her to know he had taken care of her. But it also stirred a new ache in her chest.

Tears pricked at the backs of her eyes and melancholy tugged at her emotions, threatening to pull her into a pit of misery. But she had never allowed herself to venture there before, and she would not start now. For her own sake and William's, she focused on warming some cured ham by the fire. Then she mustered down bite after bite and forced herself through her nightly routine despite the unsettling dark that had fallen around her and Goldie.

"I am sorry," she whispered to the mare as she stepped close and rubbed the horse's soft nose. "I know it is not original, but it is all I could think of." And naming the horse and hugging her big head to her chest made her feel less alone. She gave the horse's thick, snow-dampened neck one last stroke before she settled into her pile of furs, with her back against the wall of rock behind her and William's rifle gripped in her left hand. He had told her once how to shoot it, and she prayed if danger came in the night, she would be able to.

~

*L*ucinda awoke with a jerk to the rustling of leaves. Eyes wide and ears open for trouble, she scanned the world around her in a state of exhausted confusion. But as she took in the snow-covered scene, reality crashed down upon her. She was alone, William had been taken prisoner, and the horse she had named Goldie lipped at snow- and leaf-covered grass a couple of feet before her.

Slowly, her grip on the barrel of William's rifle softened. But the vice-grip around her heart did not. Instead, it pressed upward, clawing its way up her throat until it spewed forth as liquid from her eyes. She tried every trick in her arsenal to refrain from weeping. But no positive thought, no song, or no prayer could stop the tears. They flowed unchecked like a river too full for its banks. No thoughts of cold or pain penetrated her mind as the sobs racked her body. Only a deep, despairing loneliness and hopelessness. Who was she to think that she could ever save William? He might not even be alive. And here she sat, lost in the middle of the wilderness after leading her horse blindly through a land she had never encountered.

"God, I cannae do this," she cried to the heavens. "How am I supposed to do this? I am lost. I have no idea where I am or where he is. An' even if I could find him, how could I possibly save him? I cannot use the weapons in me stead. I am frail an' broken. I am not capable of these things Ye have called me to do!"

Lucinda buried her face in her hands, but her tears began to slow. For deep within her heart, a small voice whispered that her words were incorrect, that she *was* capable. She shook her head and leaned back against the rock, a fur wrapped around her shoulders. "Nay. It cannae be true."

But then again, was the Bible tucked in her saddlebag not proof that all throughout history, God had called those that were not equipped for the task? Was she not a daughter of the one true King? Yes, she remembered that night so many years ago when she had cried out in her heart for the Lord to save her and she had been answered with an overwhelming inner peace. An inner peace that had sustained her through the years. And would sustain her now. God was within her. She would not fall.

Lord, I do not know how it is possible, but I put this in Your hands. Please direct my path.

She leaned her head back against the cold rock wall and sucked in a deep breath of icy air. And she centered herself on the peaceful place within her soul, the place that knew all things were truly possible in the Lord. After all, was He not the one that made the dumb to speak and the lame to leap? Could He not do the same with her?

All she knew with certainty was that she could not do it alone. With one more deep, fortifying breath, she rose from her pile of furs and pulled some ham from her pack for sustenance. Then, when the campfire was properly extinguished, she climbed atop Goldie, her shoulders square and her chin lifted high. She closed her eyes and whispered to the heavens. "Lord, please guide our steps." Patiently and calmly, she waited and listened for some kind of sign or direction. When Goldie stepped forward, she lowered her hands and gave the horse her head, allowing her to lead.

～

Sweat beaded on William's brow and slid down his temples despite the cold air that touched his face. His shoulder burned and ached like a fiery inferno had been lit right inside his muscle and stoked to fan out to the rest of his body. Chills racked him and chattered his teeth together. A pungent odor penetrated the air from the medicine woman's foul-smelling concoction she had applied to the wound. He might be straddling death's doorstep, but all he could think of was Lucinda. And it made him suck in painful breath after painful breath of stifling, stench-filled air.

She was the only thing that kept him from drifting into ill thoughts of the crazed medicine woman who had advocated for his care. When he was drug into camp tied to a tree branch, death had only been a hair's breadth away. But the little woman with graying black hair and a wrinkled face had waved her arms wildly and jabbered words he could not decipher even in his right mind. Then the poisoned arrow had been removed from his shoulder, and rough hands had brought him into the hut where he now lay. Where he clung to the tenuous thread of life that had been afforded him, his every aching thought centered on Lucinda. Had she escaped? Was she alive? Was that why he had not seen her in camp? Initially, he had assumed the worst. But she had not been taken prisoner, so that left two options. One of which he could not bear the thought of.

A groan not related to his pain escaped from his body. Lucinda had come to mean too much to him. He had not realized how much so until he heard that war cry. The same cry that still haunted his fitful bouts of lapses into unconsciousness. Without meaning to, without even realizing it, he had fallen in love with Lucinda. With her strawberry-blond hair and her pale, freckled skin. With her quiet determination and the way she needed him, even though she would not admit it. To the feel of her body close to his in the saddle. And to the way she tried, every day, to please him. He did not deserve a woman as good and kind as her. Someone who believed in him, though she knew full well exactly how undeserving he was. But to face losing her, it tore his heart out and caused more pain than the poisoned arrow ever could.

To make matters worse, there was not a thing he could do to help Lucinda in his current condition. But somehow, through his delirium, a still small voice broke through to remind him he was not completely helpless. There was one thing he could do, and that was to pray. Though his prodigal heart balked at the idea, he was desperate and willing to do anything to ensure Lucinda's safety. So, for the first time in over five years, he ran toward the Lord with everything in him instead of away. With every coherent thought, he prayed. He prayed to the only one who could help Lucinda now. To the one who, though he did not wish to admit it, had been helping her all along.

And somehow, in those moments of lucidness, William realized his greatest fault. Errantly, due to the loss of his sister, he had taken it upon himself to shoulder all responsibility. No longer trusting in the God who had taken his sister, William had appointed himself Lucinda's personal savior and body guard. He had felt a desperate need to protect her with his own two hands, which was futile. Just as with his sister, there was nothing he could do if the Lord called Lucinda home.

He begged forgiveness and prayed to the one in whose care his wife had been all along. He thanked the Lord for blessing him with her presence and vowed that if he was allowed to see her again, he would be the best husband he could be.

~

*a*t the sight of a small, swirling puff of smoke rising into the air, Lucinda asked Goldie to halt atop the ridge. A strange mix of apprehension and hope coursed through her, sending a shiver down her spine unrelated to the frigid weather. Beneath her, the mare's shoulder rippled in anticipation. *Does the fire belong to a friend or foe, Lord?*

Lucinda waited for an answer but felt nothing save for concern and longing. Her mouth formed a line, and Goldie shifted as she gripped the reins tighter. Forcing herself to relax, she took a deep breath and stretched her spine and fingers while maintaining a loose hold on the leather. There was only one way to know what the fire meant. Yet a thousand possibilities still ran through her mind as she asked her mount to walk forward.

Strategically, Lucinda picked her way around the edge of the ridge while slowly working her way downward. She attempted to remain inconspicuous while her mind ran rampant. If the camp belonged to William's captors, what would she do? While finding him was her greatest wish, a heavy weight of dread lodged in her stomach. Though she had several weapons, she only had knowledge of William's rifle. And even then, she doubted her efficiency.

But even if whomever she found was not hostile, would they be kind to her, much less lend a hand in her cause? Her hope wavered. Her first hurdle would be simple acceptance. At least, from where she sat astride Goldie, her limp would be unapparent. And her unsightly fingers were hidden behind the fur-lined gloves of William's making. But garnering assistance? Most people in their right mind would send her on her way rather than help her infiltrate a hostile camp. Uneasiness stirred in her chest, but she focused her attention on winding down the hillside instead.

When Lucinda reached a stand of cedars she could use for cover while maintaining the high ground, she slipped from Goldie's back. Carefully picking her way over the frozen earth, she hid behind the dark, prickly branches. But as she took in the scene below her in the valley, a wave of shock washed over her, nearly knocking her backward. Brow furrowed and mouth pulled into a tight bow, she moved back to Goldie's side and swung up into the saddle. Then she lifted William's rifle and nudged the mare forward with her calves.

At the snap of a twig under the horse's hoof, the dark-headed man sitting beside the fire shifted from sitting to kneeling and whipped his own rifle around. They froze with rifles aimed at one another. "Donegal?"

Donegal's brow wrinkled before he lowered his rifle and stood. "Mrs. Cole?"

Lucinda's shoulders relaxed, but though she lowered

her own weapon, she kept it at the ready. She nodded to acknowledge his question but asked one of her own. "I thought you were…" Though she had been concerned about what became of him, a memory flashed through her mind, replayed in slow motion. She had watched him take a tomahawk to the head, watched him fall.

"Aye."

Lucinda perked at his voice, for in all the time she had traveled with the man, she had not given a thought to their common heritage. Feeling a sudden kinship, she relaxed further. What a blessing that he was alive, but how?

"They took off me ear an' left me for dead," Donegal explained as he whisked the hat from his head, revealing the makeshift bandage covering the right side. Lucinda's stomach roiled at the sight of the blood-stained cloth. "I managed to crawl away after they left."

Realization dawned. "While I was hidin'." Shame washed over Lucinda. While she had been wallowing in self-pity behind a tree, Donegal had been left to fend for himself with life-threatening injuries. Who else in such a predicament might she have overlooked? *Could I have saved someone?* She swallowed the lump that had formed in her throat. "I ran an' hid behind a tree. They must not have seen me." She shook her head.

Donegal was silent as he watched her for several moments. "Were ye the only one?"

The question came out tight, as though he did not truly want the answer. Lucinda could not blame him. It was not an answer she wished to give either. She sucked in a shaky breath. "They took three prisoners, includin' William." Tears threatened, but she blinked them back.

Donegal hung his head and gave the slightest of nods. "Well, climb on down here an' have ye a bite to eat." He motioned for her to dismount and join him, then moved to settle back by the fire.

Lucinda swung down but stopped beside Goldie's head. "Is there somewhere I can water my mare?"

The man pointed through the woods to his right. "Be careful."

~

"*I* plan to find William." Lucinda leveled her declaration at Donegal as they drank down their simple broth of chipped meat and water.

There was a long silence before Donegal finally spoke in slow, careful words. "I know where he is at."

Lucinda's eyes widened, and her stomach did a strange flop. Hope mixed with dread once again. But she kept her gaze on Donegal's face as she asked, "Ye do?"

Another silence. His jaw worked, reminding her of the very man they discussed. Her heart ached and her mouth pressed into a tight line as she awaited his response. A sigh came before his answer. "I know where the camp is. But...I have seen nothin' of the prisoners...yet."

Lucinda's heart sank. "Oh." Her voice was barely audible as she processed the news.

Donegal sighed again before his quiet confession. "I knew of the prisoners. But...I did not know how much ye knew. An' I did not want to get yer hopes up."

Lucinda nodded as tears clouded her vision. *He did not want to get me hopes up because he believes they are already dead.* She closed her eyes against the dam that risked breaking within her. She would not blindly accept his suspicion as the truth. No, she needed to see for herself before she gave up hope. Raising her chin, she kept her voice level. "Show me. Tomorrow."

CHAPTER 17

*L*ucinda and Donegal crawled on their stomachs to the edge of a cliff overlooking the small river valley where the Chickamauga camp was situated. She frowned as she peered over, and apprehension tickled the back of her neck. For here were the same people who had shot and captured William. Without their war paint, the Chickamaugae appeared more human, their daily lives resembling that of life on the trail. But the way the men strutted confidently about caused her hands to clench the dead grass at her fingertips. The men that attacked them could not possibly be human. A normal human could not commit such atrocities against one another. Could they? Yet...all the stories Lucinda had read in the Bible showed otherwise. Humans had been committing atrocious acts against one another since the beginning of time.

But always, there had been good in the world as well. God was the good, the light. So she would not let the evil diminish her hope, for it was all she had left at the moment.

Quietly and patiently, she scanned the valley before them, checking every inch, every face, for William. Thankfully, Donegal seemed in no hurry to abandon their post either. Though the longer they stared, the more Lucinda's optimism sagged. William seemed to be nowhere in sight.

Men whittled arrows from tree branches and stretched hides on frames to tan them. Women carried babies on their hips and sewed moccasins from leather. One elderly woman with hunched shoulders caught Lucinda's eyes. The woman was more lavishly dressed than most others, with countless leather pouches hanging around her thin neck. But more than her dress, or the gray tinging her tresses, her attitude set her apart. The tiny woman, short and slight in stature, stood wagging her finger up at a man more than twice her size. The tanned brave with a long black ponytail maintained his hard, stoic expression throughout her badgering.

When the woman pivoted and marched away, the man shook his head. But then he turned to a couple of other men and barked orders as he motioned toward a hut at the edge of camp, near a shallow creek. The men, still tall but not as much so as their counterpart, stood and strode in the indicated direction, entering the hut. When they re-emerged, she stifled a gasp—for with an arm draped over the shoulders of the men on either side of him was William.

Tears sprang into her eyes, and her gloved hands covered her mouth. Here indeed was the man she loved, alive and whole. Emotions flowed wildly within her as she observed his pale complexion, face distorted in pain, and obvious weakness. It took all her strength to remain still as they lowered him to a sitting position beside the campfire. Worry hammered her heart against her ribcage until she noticed the way he slumped grumpily beside the fire. Not as weak as he wanted them to think? Hope renewed within her core as a smile stretched her mouth behind her hands.

William was naked from the waist up with only a fur thrown around his shoulders. When a bowl of stew was brought to him, her frown returned. Though he cradled the wooden bowl in his right hand, he kept the arm tucked tightly against his side and ate with his left hand. His shoulder must still pain him a great deal. While she had not witnessed William with a serious injury, she had never seen him show any sign of weakness.

Thus far, he had been her mighty fortress, strong and supportive. But now, they would both have to lean upon the One True Fortress for strength and patience. For He held their future.

When Donegal poked her arm, Lucinda jerked. Wordlessly, he motioned for her to back away from their vantage point. She pursed her lips as she stole one last, lingering glance in William's direction. Then she nodded her assent and turned to crawl in the opposite direction than they had come.

Guilt and anticipation warred within her as she followed Donegal back to camp. Anxiously, she waited for him to divulge his plan. And yet, he remained irritatingly quiet. Lucinda raised a brow as he stopped by their campfire he had doused earlier, surveying their surroundings. Her hands found their way to her hips, and she was about to open her mouth to demand he share his thoughts when he spoke. "We need to act fast. But careful." He glanced at Lucinda, as if sizing her up. "How well can ye ride?"

"Well." She gave a sharp, confident nod.

"Good. This plan hinges on it. Our greatest advantage is that if they have horses, they have them hidden away from the central camp. That means they will be delayed in their pursuit. I will attempt to delay them further. Ye will ride, an' I will provide cover."

Lucinda froze. "Ye want me to rescue him?"

Donegal did not even glance up as he quickly gathered their supplies. "Aye."

An icy breeze brushed against her face, stealing her breath. Her stomach dropped, and her feet seemingly anchored to the ground. She struggled to force air into her lungs. Could it really have come to this? William's life hinging on her ability to rescue him?

She closed her eyes. No. His rescue hinged upon the one who guarded them both. When she reopened her eyes, she lifted her chin and moved alongside Donegal.

"Are there any of these yer comfortable with?" The tall, dark-headed man motioned to where several guns laid atop a fur beside their saddlebags.

Lucinda lifted the rifle in her hands. "William showed me how to shoot his." Her heart thudded in her chest. To use the term comfortable was stretching matters, considering she had never even gone through the motions William had shown her. But at least she had an inkling of how to get a shot off, should she encounter trouble. Silently, she prayed it would be enough.

"All right. You keep that one." Donegal nodded before he began strapping weapons to his body.

~

*O*nly a short time later, after having confirmed William was still in the open beside the campfire, Lucinda and Donegal stood just far enough from the Chickamauga camp to prevent being noticed. Finally, Donegal revealed the full scope of his plan.

"Watch for me to drop this bundle from the clifftop." He motioned toward the observation point they had used earlier with a rock wrapped in gray fur. "It should garner their attention an' provide a distraction. But as soon as ye see it, ride as hard an' as fast as ye can. Keep ye gun at the ready in case ye need it, an' slow only enough for William to swing up, then get out of there. Ride until yer horse cannae go any farther. Cross creeks, change directions, whatever it takes to get away an' make yerself hard to track."

Lucinda nodded at each instruction he gave, but deep inside, her confidence wavered. *Lord, please provide Your guidance and help.*

Donegal continued without notice of her hesitation. "I will provide cover from there." He inclined his head toward their earlier vantage point before he turned a serious, penetrating blue gaze upon her. "But once yer free, do not return for me. I will find ye or I will move on alone.

But I dinnae want either of ye killed tryin' to get me out of there."

Lucinda nodded, though her insides balked at the idea of leaving Donegal after he was so selflessly risking himself for William. Her mouth pressed into a line, but she could think of no immediate alternative. While her and William's lives might depend upon her following Donegal's instruction, would they simply be trading one life for another? *Lord, please not. Please keep us all safe*, she prayed as she mounted Goldie. Donegal gave her one last look as if to confirm if she were ready for the task ahead, then hurried off to his post.

Lucinda attempted to ignore the nerves that fluttered in her stomach as she watched the clifftop above the tree line. She forced air in and out of her lungs as she kept her focus sharp and her gaze intent. She had nearly come to the conclusion that she must have missed Donegal's signal when the small gray mass finally dropped alongside the cliff wall. Kissing to the mare, Lucinda leaned forward and gave Goldie a kick with both legs. As if she too had been waiting in quiet anticipation, the horse plunged straight into a run. Lucinda kept her watch on the ground ahead of them for obstacles as they sailed forward, but Goldie proved sure-footed and agile.

Within seconds, they burst through the trees and into the clearing where the camp lay. Lucinda's eyes locked on William's form, huddled by the campfire. And the eyes of the guard next to him locked on her. Lucinda's heart sank into her stomach, but still she drove forward. "William," she screamed, and his gaze snapped up to her face. His eyes widened a fraction of a second before he tucked and rolled away from the guard.

Goldie did not hesitate to run right up beside the orange flames of the campfire and even remained calm when a gunshot rang through the valley. Donegal. Lucinda's heart beat wildly in her chest, yet she reined Goldie in enough for William to mount. But when she looked in William's direction, the guard grabbed her around the waist. Without thinking, she whirled and struck him across the jaw with the barrel of the rifle. And when that did not dislodge him, she whipped the gun around and brought the butt down on top of his head. Dazed, the man loosened his hold while William mounted and kicked the man away.

For a split second, joy and relief washed through Lucinda as William settled behind her, but she had no time to relish the sensation. Another ear-splitting crack sounded over them, and Goldie leapt into action, carrying them to the edge of camp and over the shallow stream that had turned mostly to ice.

William held solid while the capable mare darted through barren woods and around stands of pine and cedar. She slowed going up hillsides, taking long, powerful strides and then kept her control on downhill slopes. Goldie carried them for miles, even crossing freezing creeks and streams in great bounds. But eventually, the mare's sides heaved, and their own breaths came heavily.

When Lucinda murmured to the horse what a good job she had done and that she could slow now, Goldie slipped into a tired, plodding walk. Lucinda turned in the saddle to ensure no one followed, and her shoulder came into contact with her husband's broad body. When relief washed over her that the escape plan had worked, she allowed herself to soak in the feel of him for a moment before she turned her attention to scanning their horizons for a safe place to make camp.

"There." William's hoarse voice spoke up from behind her.

Her gaze followed to where he indicated a rock wall. When they drew closer, she let out a soft laugh, for the wall held an opening hidden inside an inlet, just large enough for them to enter.

When Goldie balked at the dark interior, Lucinda handed the reins to William so she could quickly gather wood and start a small fire. Though it would need larger logs added, her highest priority was to get their trio settled into hiding. With a meager light penetrating the darkness, she nodded for William to enter ahead of her. Then, with one last glance over her shoulder, she coaxed the mare inside with hushed murmurs and gentle pressure. Just inside the rock wall that acted as a lip and formed a short corridor, the cave opened up into a room large enough for all three of them to sleep comfortably. Lucinda sighed a small breath of relief.

She went to work unloading and unsaddling Goldie. She stroked the mare's sweat-lathered neck and prayed the animal would remain well. "Ye did good," she whispered before she turned her attention to making a pallet for William next to the fire. As she flicked some furs out to their full length on the ground, the fire flickered. Lucinda bit her lip and continued more carefully. She refused to leave for additional wood until she was sure William would be fine without her.

A glance at him revealed that he stared at her intently. Her lips parted as she stood frozen, his golden gaze heating her from the inside out. But when her eyes lowered to his bare chest, she swallowed and quickly turned to fetch his extra shirt from the packs. Producing the tan linsey-woolsey material, she held it out to William without meeting his gaze. "Here is yer shirt. Ye rest while I fetch more firewood."

Lucinda moved to leave the cave, but William stopped her.

"I will get the firewood." Though his voice rasped when he spoke, there was still an air of authority to it. It drew Lucinda to him, and she laid a hand upon his bare arm. His skin was cool beneath her touch, but his muscles were thick and strong. Appreciation rippled through her as she looked up into the face she loved.

"Nay. Ye need to rest," Lucinda urged him. "I will be careful."

William's good hand caressed her elbow as his eyes roamed her face. He moved closer until their bodies were only a hair's breadth apart. His mouth turned down at the corners, but she recognized it was only out of concern for her well-being.

Finally, he spoke again. "Take the rifle with you."

Lucinda smiled and nodded. "I will be back directly." Then she darted from the cave.

Outside, apprehension prickled at the back of her neck. But she kept a watchful eye on her surroundings and hurriedly gathered the needed firewood.

When she returned, Lucinda nearly jumped out of her skin. William leaned against the edge of the entrance. After struggling to recover her grip on her armload, she expelled a long breath. "Ye scared me," she hissed, her eyes wide as she turned and glanced around one last time before she entered the cave. William followed close behind her, his shirt restored upon his person.

She knelt by the dissipating fire and fed it until it sprang to life again. Then William's hand touched her arm, his presence at her shoulder. When she glanced up, he caressed the side of her face. Lucinda closed her eyes as she leaned into his touch. An overwhelming joy bubbled up from deep inside, filling her eyes with happy tears. She turned away to blink back the tears without notice.

"What is wrong?" William's voice was soft as his hand dropped to her shoulder.

Lucinda faced her husband while attempting to rein in her emotions. But the sight of his familiar, handsome profile did little to abate her gratitude at having him in her life once more. "I am sorry." She shook her head, and her mouth turned up at the corners against her will. She did not wish to make a show in front of William, but her feelings could not be helped. "I am just glad to have ye back, is all."

A low growl slipped from William as he swept her into a warm embrace. Lucinda wrapped her arms around his thick middle and snuggled her head under his chin. She nestled into the strength of his body and relished how tightly he held her, as if he, too, had been scared to lose her.

"Thank you, Lord," he whispered, and she looked up at him. Her heart melted at the warmth and gratitude that shone in his hazel eyes. At the way he looked at her as if she were an incredible, invaluable prize. "Yes," he whispered. "The Lord answered my prayers when He kept you safe. And when He brought you back to me?" He shook his head in wonder.

Lucinda's heart overflowed with happiness at her husband's confession. His words worked their way deep into her soul and re-stirred her swirl of emotions. She dislodged herself from his middle and threw her arms around his neck, eliciting a grunt of pain. But as tears fell from her eyes, he simply held her tighter, if slightly one-armed. "I thought I had lost ye," she cried into his neck, ignoring the prickle against her face.

"Shh," he soothed. "I am here now."

Finally, Lucinda dried her tears and pulled away. "I am sorry." She glanced down as embarrassment flamed in her cheeks. What had come over her? Sure, her husband had expressed affection and gratitude for her presence. But it was not a declaration of love. She should have controlled her reaction. She searched for something to distract herself with and settled on the fact that she needed to start supper. "I will go find water." She started to stand, but William placed a hand on her wrist. When she glanced up at him, his expression was earnest.

"I will go."

Lucinda opened her mouth to protest but closed it. Forehead wrinkled in concern and the corners of her mouth turned down, she watched William move to the saddlebags, his arm still closely tucked into his side. He produced a couple of pots before he headed for the exit. Lucinda took a step toward him and placed a hand on his arm as he moved past.

"Be careful."

William hesitated. His eyes roamed her face, as if soaking in the view of her, and heat crept up her neck. "I will," he said huskily.

Lucinda stepped back, letting him go. Reluctantly, she returned to tending the fire and anxiously awaited William's return.

CHAPTER 18

*a*s William stepped outside, an icy wind gusted up behind him and snaked its way under his shirt. He shivered violently, causing a jolt of pain to course through his shoulder. But he had not seen hide nor hair of his leather coat since he awakened in the hut. Still, he pressed toward the last stream they had passed. He could not continue to allow his wife to handle all the duties, especially under the circumstances. There was no sign they had been followed very far, but their horse could be tracked, especially given the extra weight she had carried. As he walked, swift but careful, he watched for tracks he might need to hide but found few on the hard ground.

To his dismay, when he reached the stream, it was nearly completely frozen. The small trickle left in the center was not near wide enough to dip the pot. He frowned, for he had not brought a single tool. Glancing around, he spotted a heavy rock and grabbed it up in his left hand. When he slammed it down against the thick ice, pain reverberated through his body, causing a hiss to pass through his lips. Still, he raised the rock and hammered it against the ice again and again until he broke through. Then he scooped two pots full. Ignoring the pain that ripped through his shoulder and radiated outward, he held one in each hand as he started his slow trek back to the cave. His energy waning, he prayed he would arrive at his destination.

Finally, he made it to the cave opening and dragged his weary feet onto the stone. As he did so, his toe collided with a rock and sent it skidding deeper into the cave. The action must have scared Lucinda, who waited near the entrance, for utter alarm passed over her face before it was replaced with a relieved smile. Without a word, he handed one pot of water to her and took the other to the mare.

When he turned around, a smile quirked his wife's lips. Too worn out to contemplate what she might have found amusing, he simply took solace in her joy and settled next to her on the furs as she started her meal preparation. Lucinda poured them each a cup of water before she added chipped ham to the pot of water for a broth. Slowly, he reached for his cup and brought the cold liquid to his lips. Its freezing tendrils seared down his parched throat in a closer resemblance to fire than ice.

Cocking his head as a memory slipped back, he addressed his wife. "Are we expecting company?" His brows knit together as he attempted to form thoughts and piece memories together.

Lucinda glanced up at him, her own brow wrinkled in confusion.

"Someone provided cover for us back there," he added to explain his illogical comment.

His wife's expression fell, and her mouth turned down in a frown, making him wish he had not spoken.

"That was Donegal. But I dinnae know when or if he will find us." She shook her head, her face grim. "He said to get ye to safety, an' he might find us if he could."

William gave a solemn nod. Another question came to mind, but he almost did not want to make the inquiry. He had seen enough destruction before he lost consciousness to deduce the answer. But he had to know. "Did...did anyone else make it?"

Lucinda faced him again, her eyes shining with tears in the gathering dusk of the cave. "Nay. Just us. An' Donegal lost an ear." Her chin wobbled, and he thought she would start to cry again, but she held fast. Blinking back her tears, she turned back to the pot and stirred the simmering broth.

His chest constricted with compassion for his wife. Setting his cup to the side, William scooted closer and pulled her into his embrace once more.

As she continued her rhythmic motion with the ladle, Lucinda leaned into him. It was a nearly imperceptible difference in her posture, but it brought William a comfort that outweighed the sadness that shadowed the moment. And reminded him that through the trials, God still had a plan.

As he admired the way the soft, strawberry-blond wisps of hair curled around her ears and the creaminess of her skin, his emotions rekindled. No matter how difficult, he needed to be honest with his wife. Though deep down he knew she cared as deeply for him as he did for her, a thread of worry still wound through him. *Will she truly respond as well as I hope?* The thought was almost a silent plea to the heavens.

With a deep, fortifying breath, William removed the pot from the fire and coaxed Lucinda around to face him. Her light-gray-blue eyes were wide and wary as she looked up at him.

"Lucinda, I...I want a real marriage with you."

Her lips parted, and even in the dim lighting, the pink that crept up her neck and over her cheeks was visible. "Ye do?"

William took her hands in his. "Yes. I do. If...if that would please you." He inclined his head toward her in question.

Much to his great pleasure, a broad smile spread across Lucinda's face. Then, as she once again blinked back tears, she nodded emphatically. The joy that radiated from her stirred an indescribable happiness within William's soul.

He reached up and caressed her cheek, skin on skin. A lone tear slipped down Lucinda's face, but a smile still stretched her lips. With the love and warmth that radiated from her gaze, he could not help leaning in and pressing a kiss to her lips.

Cold at first, their lips quickly warmed as they joined. Lucinda leaned into him, into his touch, and into his kiss. A low moan of pleasure rumbled from his throat as he soaked in the soft, sweet feel of her lips against his. Between them, he sensed a melding of their spirits as well as their bodies. Their very souls intertwined in a beautiful show of vulnerability. A perfect intimacy of husband and wife.

When William pulled away, his breath shallow, he kept a hand on the soft skin of Lucinda's jaw and rested his forehead against hers. He closed his eyes and savored the moment until the popping of the fire finally drew their attention. He sat back as Lucinda returned to her previous task. Within moments, they both held a cup of broth, relishing in the liquid's warmth in addition to each other's company.

Finally, William broke the silence. The need to be clear and establish expectations weighed heavily on his heart. "Listen," he began. Lucinda looked up at him through her tawny lashes. "I do not know exactly what a genuine marriage will look like for us." He hesitated. "But however it is, I want it to be rooted in love." He touched her elbow, drawing the full force of her gaze.

Lucinda offered him a soft smile. "Of course." She squeezed his hand.

But he did not let go, and she did not pull her hand from his. So they continued their meal in contented silence, hand in hand.

~

William's brows furrowed as he awoke the next morning. Slowly, he oriented himself to his surroundings. The cool, damp cave. The incessant, annoying pain in his shoulder that he welcomed only because it meant he was alive. And the beautiful woman lying at his side. The corners of his mouth rose slowly as he took in her peaceful face. The braid she had fashioned her hair into the night before lay over her shoulder, its reddish-golden hues catching the light that trickled in from the mouth of the cave. A few stray wisps framed her face. Her skin was pale, but in a way that mimicked fragile porcelain. The color, complete with freckles, suited his wife. Though she might be physically frail, she had character and strength. And her petite body melded perfectly with his. Just the way God intended it. His heart swelled with joy. To think that only a couple months before, he had not been truly aware of her existence. And that only a week before, he had still fought his feelings for her. But the attack had showed him what was important, what he should cling to.

So he did. As morning dawned, he propped up on his elbow and admired his wife, with his right arm carefully draped over her slender body. He listened to the sweet sound of her soft breathing as her ribs slowly raised and lowered his arm. How blessed he was. So lost in the moment's peace was he that he nearly forgot why they laid on the hard floor of a cave with barely enough supplies to see them through.

Slowly, responsibility worked its way into his chest and settled there with its pressing weight. He needed to get them to safety, far away from those who had massacred their travel party. His heart hurt, and his gaze returned to his sleeping wife's face. Could he ever truly ensure her safety? Kentucky was wild country. But it would be just as dangerous to travel back the way they had come alone. Sure, he had traveled that route for years. But that was when he had only been risking himself.

When he had not cared if he lived or died. Now he had a
wife to care for. To live for. Indecision weighed heavily
on him.

But as he stared down at his wife, a gentle reminder of
the one who could keep her safe nudged his spirit. *Forgive
me again, Oh, Lord.* William nestled his head against
Lucinda's as he prayed. *I thank You for bringing her back to
me, the most precious blessing. Greater than anything I could
have imagined. But I place her in Your hands. I have tried to
assume control of her care, Lord, but though I may try my best,
I am only a man. You are the only one truly capable of her care.
And I pray for her safety. I ask that our days together are
many, Lord, and I promise to count each as a blessing. I pray
for Your direction, Lord. Please lead us down Your path.*

William sat in the silence a few moments longer,
listening for direction. But his concentration was interrupted when Lucinda's breathing stuttered before a deep
inhalation. She smacked her mouth as if it were dry and
nestled deeper into him, restoring the curve to his lips.
Then her brows lowered and her eyes blinked open. The
wrinkle in her forehead relaxed, and the corners of her
eyes crinkled as she smiled up at him. "Good mornin',"
she greeted him, her voice soft and raspy.

"Good morning." He cringed at the hoarseness of his
own voice.

But Lucinda's smile only stretched farther. Then, as
she wormed away from him to stretch out her limbs
before she rose, her eyes closed, and pain pulled her
mouth into a frown and curled her nose. It tugged at
William's heart. If only he could ease her pain.

He did the only thing he could think of instead. He

averted his attention, stretching his own joints and muscles as he gave his wife her privacy. Then he spoke. "I think we should stay one more day here. In case Donegal comes to find us."

Lucinda nodded her agreement. She looked toward the saddlebags, undoubtedly concerned about supplies. But he would not leave her to hunt. Not yet. Not this close to those who had already harmed them. "I think I will step outside a moment for fresh air."

William extended a hand to stay her. "Let me go first." She rolled her lip under, and he understood her urgency to handle morning matters. But he had to ensure her safety. "I will be back momentarily," he assured her. Lucinda nodded, but when he picked up his rifle and walked to the edge of the cave, she followed.

"Be careful," she whispered before he stepped out into the sunlight.

"I will." He smiled and bent for a kiss.

CHAPTER 19

While broth and cured ham still comprised their only meals for the day, Lucinda contributed a delicious pine tea to break the monotony.

"Mmm," William rumbled next to her. "Where have you been hiding this secret?" He raised an eyebrow as he addressed her in that deep voice that warmed her so.

A smile lifted the corners of her lips as she took in his admiring gaze. Without his hat, his disheveled hair fell every which way across his head, creating sandy waves. The cave was dark, but firelight flickered across his tan skin and hazel eyes in wonderful golden hues. Warmth filled her chest and overflowed to the rest of her body.

How satisfying that such a simple gesture should please him. Her smile turned wry as she lifted one shoulder in a shrug. "I had not thought of it before. I have not had it since I was a little girl." She shook her head as she turned to gaze into the orange flames before them.

William was silent for a moment. "I am sorry."

Lucinda offered him a growing smile. For as she stared in his face with love filling her heart, the pain of the past did not carry the sting it once did, because she no longer felt lonely or unloved. Not only had she found companionship, but her life held possibility and purpose. Though she knew not what the next day would hold, or if they would even survive the week, they were together. And God was in control.

"Dinna fash yerself," she finally replied softly. "I am simply glad I remembered." She held up her tin cup before she took a sip. The liquid slipped down her throat and heated her stomach. With it came the comfort of a long-forgotten memory with her mother, of sipping the stout drink as they sat near a fireplace, reading. Warmth seemed to envelop her as she closed her eyes and immersed herself in the memory. When she reopened them, she leaned against William's shoulder, soaking in his nearness. He leaned over and dropped a kiss on top of her head, sending tingles all the way down to her toes. The moment felt perfect, as if they would never need anything more than the here and now.

Fear tried to worm its way into Lucinda's soul, and she let out a sigh. William seemed to sense the emotion stirring inside her and fighting for space because he set his cup to the side and turned toward her. The serious set of his jaw caused her heart to kick into double time. "What is it?"

William's face softened, and he sweetly caressed her cheek. "Nothing too serious, my dear. I only wish to know where you desire to make our home."

Lucinda blinked and tilted her head to the side before

her brow furrowed. "What do ye mean? I thought we were to make our home here in Kentucky."

She watched William's expression as he took a deep breath and released it. The knot of tension in her stomach remained in place until he spoke. "Given recent events, I wanted to see if you would rather stay in Kentucky or go back East. I could take you to meet my parents if they are still living." The corner of his mouth quirked up, and the light in his eyes made him look like a boy again. Then he hesitated, and the joy slipped from his face once more. "But both choices seem wrought with danger." William took both of her hands into his. "And I only wish to keep you safe. So I thought I would leave the choice for you."

Lucinda's heart melted. Firelight flickered across William's face as well as the cave walls around them, creating dancing shadows. A knot of emotion swelled in her throat and made it difficult to speak. For the first time in her life, someone put her consideration, her wants and needs, above all else. William wanted her opinion and input. The thought warmed her cheeks and set a smile to her face.

She withdrew her hands from his and placed them on each side of the scruffy, pock-marked face she had come to love so dearly. "William, I would be happy to live with ye anywhere." Lucinda motioned to the rock walls around them. "Even in a cave. To be with ye, to have a marriage an' someone who cares for me..." She blinked back tears as she shook her head. "It is all I could ever ask for."

In response, William scooped her up with his good arm and drew her into his lap. He wrapped the other arm loosely around her and nestled his face into her neck. A happy groan escaped his body before he brought his head up. "I love you, Lucinda."

Her mouth fell open as she gaped up at her husband, emotion stirring in her chest. "Ye do?" When she finally managed to string those two words together, they were not the ones she had meant to say. Not the ones that her heart sang with.

William chuckled that low, hearty sound she enjoyed so before he nodded, his face dipping closer to her. "Yes, darlin'. It only took me a while to admit it."

"I love ye too." Lucinda rushed to bring her mouth up to his as tears of happiness dampened her lashes. She pressed into him, allowing all of her love and emotion to flow through that single act of passion. William responded accordingly, pulling her against him and bringing a hand up to cradle her neck. Her body melded with his like the perfect halves of a whole. His lips were both pliant and coaxing in the melodious harmony of a song only God could create.

A rustle outside the cave shattered the moment. William quickly removed her from his lap and spun for his rifle. Grabbing it up, he brought it to his shoulder and angled it toward the dark opening. As he crept across the pale limestone floor, Lucinda wanted to reach out to him, to stop him but instead, it was as though her feet were anchored in place. Her heart beating rapidly, she prayed that there was no genuine threat, only a rabbit or other critter. When William was several feet from the cave opening, a "hoo hoo" drifted in on the breeze. William pressed his back against the wall, his brows coming together. Finally, he puckered his lips and reciprocated the call.

Lucinda held her breath and waited. Was it friend or foe out in the darkness? Or could it be an actual owl? Another rustle followed, and a chill ran down her spine. Then William snapped his rifle into place at his shoulder, aiming at the tall form of a human that appeared at the entrance of the cave.

The breath swooshed out of Lucinda's lungs and her shoulders sagged as she recognized Donegal's lean face. But William stayed frozen like stone, his gun still trained on the man.

Donegal's hands were raised beside his head, with his palms out. "I am alone."

At the answer to the unspoken question that passed between the two men, William gave a nod and lowered his rifle. But he kept an eye on the cave opening as he motioned for Donegal to join them by the fire. Only after a moment did William join them. He picked up his cup of pine tea and handed it to Donegal. "Here. Have a drink."

Donegal nodded and brought the warm liquid to his dry, cracked lips. He swallowed hard, pain etched across his face. Then, as the drink settled, his eyes closed and his shoulders relaxed. But his hands trembled each time he lifted the cup for a long sip. After several moments of silence, he glanced between William and Lucinda. "Yer not easy to find." The tiniest hint of a smile tugged at one corner of his mouth.

William relaxed visibly, his own mouth tipping up at the edges. "Good."

But her husband's expression sobered again as he took

in Donegal's appearance. The difficulty the man had encountered as he traversed the frozen Kentucky country-side was evident. His hair was riffled and his eyes haggard and haunted. Both his hat and bandage were missing, and the opening of his ear was covered in dark, crusted blood. Dirt was smeared across his cheek and neck. But he stared silently into the fire. Finally, as Lucinda stood and moved to their packs, his quiet voice broke through the silence of the cave.

"We cannot linger here long."

William nodded his understanding. "We will leave at first light."

Lucinda hesitated. She took in each of the men before her, her eyes wide. "Are either of ye well enough?"

William and Donegal exchanged glances before her husband turned to her, his face determined. He gave her a firm nod, his hazel eyes fixed on hers. Lucinda's lips pressed together, but she dipped her chin in agreement, anyway. Then she turned to the saddlebags to begin with stew preparation.

While it was dangerous to remain where they were, worry still gnawed at her stomach. William had seemed strong enough over the past couple of days, but he still favored his shoulder. Lucinda swallowed against the lump forming in her throat. She had only just gotten her husband back, and she was not ready to lose him again.

And Donegal did not appear ready for travel in the least. But neither he nor her husband would ever admit to such. All she could do was tend to their needs and pray the Lord kept them safe.

With a deep breath, Lucinda forced a smile onto her

face as she addressed Donegal. "Let me tend that ear for ye, an' then I will start the stew." She dipped the edge of a clean cloth into the pot of water.

Donegal's head swiveled quickly in her direction. His blue eyes were wide as he held out his hand. "I can clean meself up."

Lucinda hesitated, but his gaze pleaded with her. "All right," she conceded before handing him the dampened cloth. "Just let me know if there is any way I can help."

She could not have proceeded without at least making the offer. Her eyes flicked up to William's face before she settled in beside the fire. His gaze was still trained on Donegal, though his wariness had been replaced with concern.

$\sim$

*L*ucinda stifled a groan as she mounted Goldie. With pursed lips, she frowned at the stubborn men flanking her before she asked the horse to walk on. Each had insisted that she, the healthiest of the three despite her characteristic limp, ride their only mount while they walked. Neither would admit weakness, and she prayed their pride would not prove their downfall.

However, at least their fur cloaks would provide warmth. William had been sensible enough to sacrifice two of their furs for the task the night before. But the hooded cloaks also hid their weaknesses as Lucinda rode above them, and worry gnawed at her stomach as they set out.

While William had attempted to use his right arm normally since Donegal's arrival, Lucinda had noticed the flashes of pain that flared across his face and how he still favored it from time to time. And though Donegal remained stoic as well, he had slept fitfully the night before and risen with circles under his eyes even darker than those of the previous day. Though he seemed rejuvenated by assuming the role of protector alongside William, there was a weariness in his blue eyes that could not be ignored.

Lord, please protect them and give them strength.

The day was as bleak as their situation felt, with cold, thick air and low clouds. Wind howled through the trees, but Lucinda attempted to push the eerie sound to the back of her mind as she listened for danger. William had taken up another rifle made in the same style as his—the name for which she failed to remember—and allowed her to carry his in the saddle. The fact that he wanted her to be as safe as possible warmed her heart.

Indeed, she had the Lord's protection and guidance, as well as her husband's love carrying her through. And truly, that was all she needed as they headed west. William and Donegal had both decided it was best to continue the original travel plan along what was becoming known as the Kentucky Road. These trails would lead them into south central Kentucky where both William and Donegal had done much hunting and trapping. And also, where protective caves were abundant.

A smile tugged at the corner of Lucinda's mouth. She could not be sure of the third member of their party, but she and William were ready to follow where the Lord led.

That was the unspoken agreement that had passed between them that morning when the group had unanimously agreed to continue deeper into Kentucky. William's hazel gaze had been confident and loving as it met and held hers. And had carried a thousand promises of a future hoped and longed for.

A small ray of hope for the world of opportunity before them still shone in her heart. It had to. After all, each day she was blessed to continue on the journey, she lived, truly lived. So she would trust in the Lord's plan and ride with her chin held high, for as long as she was allowed.

CHAPTER 20

*W*illiam's frown deepened with each hour that passed with no shelter. Icy sleet pelted their bodies as they pressed forward step after grueling step, their fingers and toes dangerously numb. But under the present conditions, they could not stop without a proper site to shield them from the elements.

Would even finding shelter be enough? Six days had passed since they had emerged from the cave and set their path westward. And in as many days, the only spoils of hunting they could boast were two thin rabbits. As the winter drew heavy and unrelenting, game and supplies had grown scarce. If they could not locate a cave before dark, none of them would make it through the night.

Or course he would do all he could for Lucinda, guarding her with his own body, but she had grown shockingly thin. Even her face seemed gaunt despite the cheerful smile she pressed onto her lips for his benefit. It made his heart ache to watch her, malnourished, exposed to the snow and freezing winds that plagued them in turns. And now this torment of ice had set upon them with a vengeance. William attempted to resist the wracking shivers. 'Twas almost more than a body could take.

He slipped on a patch of ice-covered leaves but managed to right himself before he went down. The clear, slippery substance coated even the rugged terrain of the hills and hollers at this point, making travel all the more difficult. As if to drive home the point, Goldie's rump suddenly slid under her.

William's eyes widened, but Lucinda threw herself against the mare's neck and held on for dear life until the animal had clumsily righted itself. A renewed ache pressed into his heart. He could let nothing happen to his precious wife or the animal she had grown so fond of. No. It was not in his hands. Turning his gaze heavenward despite the stinging ice that pelted his face, he made a plea to the Lord. *Please help us. Please guide us to shelter.*

William returned his watchful eye to the forest as he pressed forward. He clenched his teeth against their involuntary chattering and instead focused on drawing steadying breaths of cold air into his lungs, scanning for shelter. But visibility was reduced, and one barren tree seemed no different than the next, with nothing to be seen past one or two trees deep. Despair threatened to take hold.

Suddenly, Donegal's voice broke through the pinging of ice against the already ice-coated trees. "There."

William followed where his arm pointed from under his fur-lined cloak. He could see little through the endless gray of dusk besides more gray, but he and Lucinda both followed blindly, led by the tiny shred of hope offered by their comrade and the sheer will to survive. And as they followed, slowly, a form began to take shape before them —the dark, open mouth of a cave. Relief washed over William and propelled him forward at a faster clip. He took hold of Goldie's bridle and brought her along beside him. Outside the cave opening, he stopped and reached up to help his wife down.

She slid right into his arms, wincing as her feet hit the ground. "Th-thank ye," she breathed through clenched, chattering teeth.

The sound tore through him like a knife and without concern for the mare, he whisked Lucinda up into his arms and carried her into the darkness. A few feet inside, he carefully lowered her to the ground and went back for the mare. After guiding the animal out of the elements, he pulled out the wood they had blessedly thought to add to their packs at the first sign of poor weather.

Within minutes of them setting foot inside the cave, a small fire had sprang to life. William laid an extra fur over his wife's shoulders before braving the icy rain once more. The additional wood he collected would be laid around the fire to dry out for later use. And judging by the conditions, they would need a substantial amount.

As William pressed through the elements and searched the frozen forest floor, he prayed again that God would see them through. But at least for now, they had shelter and enough wood to keep them warm for a short time. All he could do was focus on those blessings and continue to pray. It still seemed strange to leave all in unseen hands. But then again, it released a portion of the burden from himself and also allowed him to trust in an unwavering hope.

Yes, the God above had taken his sister, a fact he would never understand. But that same God had brought Lucinda into his life, and for that, he would be forever grateful. So he withstood the cold as long as he could, then took his armload of wood back to the cave. His shoulder still ached, but compared to the ache that blanketed his entire body, it was of little consequence. He could not imagine the pain his wife must be experiencing.

When he reached the mouth of the cave, he nearly stumbled over the couple of pots that had been set out in the driving rain to collect water. His widened gaze rose to Lucinda. She pulled her mouth into a line that he could only surmise was meant as a smile, though her eyes appeared dull gray as she continued to shake. And here he had thought her almost insensible from the cold when he had laid her in the cave. Admiration swelled in his chest and propelled him forward. Quickly, he arranged the wood to dry.

As he turned to survey the scene around him, his heart filled with wonder. Not only had his wife set the pots out for water in the time he was away, but she had also loosed every fur from the saddle. She and Donegal already huddled in cocoons of fur on either side of the fire. As she caught his eye, Lucinda lifted an arm, inviting him into the warmth of her larger cocoon.

William slipped inside. He pulled his wife close before he wrapped the furs tightly around them. And as his limbs began to painfully thaw, he focused on her slight body nestled next to his and reminded himself that the pain only meant the tissues were still alive.

~

"*A*re ye sure ye will not stay?" Lucinda's brows lowered as she followed Donegal to Goldie's side.

"Aye. While the weather has eased, I need to be on me way. I dinnae wish to impose on ye an' William any longer." Donegal's eyes lifted to where William stood at the horse's head and then lowered to the task of securing his furs and saddlebag. He had taken little in the way of supplies, which only deepened Lucinda's concern. Though there was no snow or sleet outside the mouth of the cave today, the air was still frigid and promised more to come.

"Yer not an imposition." Lucinda tried once more to convince him. "If—" Her voice cracked as she made her next point. "If the attack had not happened, we would all still be traveling together." A knot formed in the middle of her throat at the thought of those left behind.

But Donegal simply shook his head. "Nay. The plan was always to reach our destination an' go about our lives. Ye an' William will have a home here once the weather turns in the spring. An' we found that little fortified homestead over the ridge. The Glover's agreed to provide any assistance they could an' will help ye establish yer homestead in the spring. But it is time for me to move on."

Lucinda bit her bottom lip and turned to William. She attempted to plead with her expression for his assistance.

But though concerned lines were etched across his face, he only lifted a shoulder in response, as if he, too, was at a loss. So she stepped back and watched as Donegal finished his preparations and gave them both one last glance before he led Goldie to the mouth of the cave. Then, without another word, he mounted and set off into the overcast morning.

Though she knew Donegal needed the horse more than she and William, her heart still ached to see Goldie go. And when she felt William's presence at her elbow, she turned and buried her face in his sturdy chest. Lucinda wrapped her arms around him and squeezed tightly.

"I am sorry, darlin'." William apologized in his deep voice, his chest vibrating against her ear before he lowered a kiss to the top of her head.

She sighed and pulled back as she looked up into his face, still clouded in concern. "Why would he not stay?"

William's lips pulled into a thin line, and his gaze followed Donegal's path away from them. "Maybe he is running from something, like I once was." His grip tightened around Lucinda, and she leaned into him as Goldie's flaxen tail disappeared into the hazy woods.

Perhaps it was so. Her chest ached with tenderness for their missing comrade. *Lord, please protect him, and bring him the same peace You have brought my husband.* She sighed as she allowed her weight to press into William.

But after a moment, he lifted her away. "I do not wish to leave you alone, but I need to take advantage of the break in weather and attempt to hunt."

Lucinda's heart dipped, and she gave him a sad smile before she nodded her understanding. She stepped close and lifted onto her toes. Meaning to plant a kiss on his cheek above the sandy-brown stubble, she was pleasantly surprised when he brought his lips to hers in a warm kiss that heated her down to her toes and lifted her spirits. And when he pulled back, the passion in his gaze promised future kisses. Her cheeks flushed, and she turned away. She moved to stoke the fire while William pulled on his fur-lined cloak and collected his rifle. Then he came to bid her farewell. "Be careful," she reminded him earnestly.

"Of course." He leaned in and pressed a soft kiss to her forehead.

She wrapped her arms around herself and watched him go. *Lord, please watch over him and allow the fruits of his efforts to be plentiful.*

An hour and a single shot later, William returned with a wonderful surprise in tow. Lucinda gasped at the sight of the small buck. "Oh, what a blessing." She clasped her hands together as he approached.

"Indeed," he agreed. "I could hardly believe my eyes when I saw him."

Lucinda glanced up and returned his knowing smile. For the time being, they would have sufficient food stores to see them through. And maybe, with the Lord's help, they would be blessed to see spring.

CHAPTER 21

March 18, 1780

*L*ucinda blinked against the morning sun as she stepped from the mouth of the cave and stretched her arms heavenward. A smile spread across her lips at the sight of the beautiful rays filtering through the trees, covered in purple buds and green emerging leaves. Though the air still held a chill, it was nothing compared to the frigid temperatures which they had endured during their trip westward or that had kept them snowbound for weeks at a time through the winter. Instead, the sun thawed her as it kissed her skin, while the cool air that brushed her cheeks revived her with its refreshing touch. Lucinda took a deep breath and released it as her grin stretched wider.

At the crunch of a twig down the steep hillside, the handsome figure that strode toward her drew her gaze. His moccasin-covered feet made little noise over the forest floor where green sprigs spouted from between the dead leaves of the passing winter. Her heart warmed at the sight of him, especially the broad grin that beamed in her direction. "Rabbit stew for supper," he announced jovially as he drew near her, his spoils of hunting slung over his shoulder and his rifle in the other hand.

"Mmm." Lucinda's stomach gurgled and her mouth salivated at the thought of such a plentiful meal. Over the hard winter, food had been even scarcer than those last days on the trail. At times, it had been only prayers and melted snow that saw them through. But the emerging spring had proved a blessing and soon, William assured her, she would be able to hunt for wild onions, mushrooms, edible plants, and herbs.

After reaching her side, William leaned down and planted a warm, lingering kiss on her lips. He drew back just a hair. "Let me drop this in the cave, and then I have something to show you."

Lucinda brought her gaze up to meet his hazel eyes, which bore into her with heat yet twinkled with gleeful mischievousness. Her mouth quirked. "Sure." She nodded and clasped her hands in front of her.

Though the changing weather brought a fresh wave of pain to her joints, it was wonderful to leave her gloves behind in the cave. She stretched her fingers and patiently waited for her husband to return and reveal his surprise. Anticipation thrummed through her as she rocked back and forth on her feet. Her thin, worn skirts swished to and fro with her movement, rustling against the tiny shoots of grass at her feet.

William reappeared seconds later, still sporting a wry

grin. Without leather to work with, he had been unable to fashion a new hat, but Lucinda did not complain. Though he would need one soon to protect him from the sun and elements, the opportunity to admire his face and hair through the winter, even running her hands through the soft locks on every occasion she could, had proven quite a boon. Her own wry smile found its place on her lips as she took his hand and followed him down the hill and off to their left. At the base of the steep hill lay the Green River, and she looked forward to making their home closer to its bank or along one of the many streams that fed into it.

As she followed along behind William, they crossed over the tiny trickle of one such spring which sprouted right from the earth itself. What a wondrous countryside God had planted them in. Lucinda sighed contentedly as she took in the scenery she had only begun to truly appreciate and explore. Across the valley, more hills rose from the banks of the Green River, stretching upward toward the bright blue spring sky. The same mix of coniferous and deciduous trees dotted their hillsides, providing a beautiful canvas of both deep and lighter green tones, as well as purple buds. And patches of stunning flowers that resembled little yellow cups and saucers could be seen in every direction. Lucinda had already plucked a handful of the sweet-smelling blooms and placed them in a tin cup to liven up their cave interior. It made her smile and reminded her of God's handiwork every time she glanced their way.

The bouquet also provided a reminder that to everything there was a season. No matter how difficult one season of life might be, the tides would indeed turn in

God's perfect time. Just as the tide had turned when God had brought the amazing man leading her through the countryside into her life. And just as the long, difficult winter had finally given way to spring, every bloom and bud was a promise from God. Lucinda's heart overflowed with gratitude.

Her smile danced upon her lips as the gurgle of water met her ears in a song as sweet as any she had ever heard. When William stopped, she drew up next to him, brought her loose hand up to his forearm, and snuggled against him. "Listen," she whispered as she closed her eyes and reveled in the peaceful morning. A robin's song mixed with babbling water, and leaves rustled as gray squirrels scavenged for acorns. Lucinda released a contented sigh.

William gave a low rumble of appreciation as well before he turned and pulled her into his embrace. "It is wonderful," he agreed reverently, wrapping his arms around her middle. "And I took it all for granted before I met you."

Lucinda smiled up at her husband. "An' I never would have encountered any of it without ye." Heat stirred in her heart and traveled up her neck, bringing a flush to her cheeks. William leaned in and placed a soft, loving kiss against her lips, causing her to lift onto her toes as she leaned into him.

"The Lord blessed me the day He brought you into my life," William murmured huskily. "And I only wish to continue to show you all this life has to offer. Starting with this." He raised a brow as he turned to the side, making a wide sweep with his arm.

On a relatively level hillside, across the short green

grass of spring and surrounded by the yellow flowers that brought her joy, logs had been laid to mark where their cabin would stand. Lucinda's heart leapt into her throat, and tears welled in her eyes. Her hand went to her mouth as a surprised gasp slipped from her body. Eyebrows raised in question, she turned to William to confirm the meaning of his surprise.

He nodded, and a proud smile stretched across his face, sparking golden light into his hazel eyes. "If you approve of the location and size, I will start on it today."

Lucinda turned her gaze back out across the meadow, spotted by sunshine and shadow, and her eyes brimmed with joyful tears. "Oh, William, it is perfect." In fact, perfect did not begin to explain how wonderful the plan was. A cabin, a home, built by the hands of the man who loved her, meant for the two of them to share for all their days. Never in her wildest dreams would she ever have thought such blessings possible.

Lucinda leaned into William's broad, hard chest, into his strength, as his arms came around her once more. His heartbeat joined the chorus of sounds she could close her eyes and bask in forever. *Thank ye, Lord.* She sent up the simple prayer, infused with heartfelt gratitude.

The Lord had blessed her beyond measure, and without a doubt, she would spend the rest of her days thanking Him. Months prior, she had prayed for Him to guide them to a land where they could live peaceably. She could think of no place more peaceful. Or magnificent.

Though their days would always hold uncertainty, the Lord had brought them thus far, and He would continue to see them through. Of that, she could be certain. And in the meantime, they would count their blessings each and every day, including every ray of sunshine and every bloom in the meadow. Lucinda glanced up into the face she had come to love so dearly. *And every kiss.* A smile stretched her mouth as she pushed onto her toes to meet her husband's lips with hers.

Did you enjoy this book? We hope so!
Would you take a quick minute to leave a review where you purchased the book?
It doesn't have to be long. Just a sentence or two telling what you liked about the story!

Receive a FREE ebook and get updates when new Wild Heart books release: https://wildheartbooks.org/ newsletter

Don't miss the next book in the Frontier Hearts Series!

By Andrea Byrd

ABOUT THE AUTHOR

Andrea Byrd is a Christian wife and mom located in rural Kentucky, who loves to spend time with her family in the great outdoors, one with nature. Often described as having been born outside her time, she has a deep affinity for an old-fashioned, natural lifestyle.

With a degree in Equine Health & Rehabilitation gathering dust and a full-time job tethering her to a desk eight hours a day, Andrea decided it was time to show both herself and her children that it is truly possible to make your dreams come true. Now with over 1,000 contemporary Christian romance novellas sold, Andrea is pursuing her passion of writing faith-filled romance woven with a thread of true history.

AUTHOR'S NOTE

First, I would like to thank you for taking the time to read William and Lucinda's story. My hope is not only that you enjoyed it, but that it revealed a bit of history to you as well. This story was inspired by my own ancestors, and countless others, that made the arduous journey through the Cumberland Gap to settle in Kentucky. Those brave souls opened up a whole new world, and for some of us, established the area in which their family to live for generations to come. Not only did I wish to honor those men and women, but to bring light to the "Hard Winter" of 1779-1780 and to those that suffer from chronic illness each and every day.

If you enjoyed this book and wish to learn more about my writing, please join my Facebook reader's group, The Reader's Nest, where all lovers of Christ-centered romance can find a home.

You can find it at:

https://www.facebook.com/groups/374798130264410/

WANT MORE?

If you love historical romance, check out the other Wild Heart books!

Marisol ~ Spanish Rose by Elva Cobb Martin

Escaping to the New World is her only option...Rescuing her will wrap the chains of the Inquisition around his neck.

Marisol Valentin flees Spain after murdering the nobleman who molested her. She ends up for sale on the indentured servants' block at Charles Town harbor—dirty, angry, and with child. Her hopes are shattered, but she must find a refuge for herself and the child she carries. Can this new land offer her the grace, love, and security she craves? Or must she escape again to her only living relative in Cartagena?

Captain Ethan Becket, once a Charles Town minister, now sails the seas as a privateer, grieving his deceased wife. But when he takes captive a ship full of indentured servants, he's intrigued by the woman whose manners seem much more refined than the average Spanish serving girl. Perfect to become governess for his young son. But when he sets out on a quest to find his captured sister, said to be in Cartagena, little does he expect his new Spanish governess to stow away on his ship with her six-month-old son. Yet her offer of help to free his sister is too tempting to pass up. And her beauty, both inside and out, is too attractive for his heart to protect itself against—until he learns she is a wanted murderess.

As their paths intertwine on a journey filled with danger, intrigue, and romance, only love and the grace of God can overcome the past and ignite a new beginning for Marisol and Ethan.

~

Rocky Mountain Redemption by Lisa J. Flickinger

A Rocky Mountain logging camp may be just the place to find herself.

To escape the devastation caused by the breaking of her wedding engagement, Isabelle Franklin joins her aunt in the Rocky Mountains to feed a camp of lumberjacks cutting on the slopes of Cougar Ridge. If only she could out run the lingering nightmares.

Charles Bailey, camp foreman and Stony Creek's itinerant pastor, develops a reputation to match his new nickname — Preach. However, an inner battle ensues when the details of his rough history threaten to overcome the beliefs of his young faith.

Amid the hazards of camp life, the unlikely friendship growing between the two surprises Isabelle. She's drawn to Preach's brute strength and gentle nature as he leads the ragtag crew toiling for Pollitt's Lumber. But when the ghosts from her past return to haunt her, the choices she will make change the course of her life forever—and that of the man she's come to love.

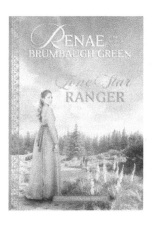

Lone Star Ranger by Renae Brumbaugh Green

Elizabeth Covington will get her man.

And she has just a week to prove her brother isn't the murderer Texas Ranger Rett Smith accuses him of being. She'll show the good-looking lawman he's wrong, even if it means setting out on a risky race across Texas to catch the real killer.

Rett doesn't want to convict an innocent man. But he can't let the Boston beauty sway his senses to set a guilty man free. When Elizabeth follows him on a dangerous trek, the Ranger vows to keep her safe. But who will protect him from the woman whose conviction and courage leave him doubting everything—even his heart?

CPSIA information can be obtained
at www.ICGtesting.com
Printed in the USA
JSHW012127280423
41028JS00004B/139

9 781942 265702